Rajmati

[Reimagined]

JENISHA MANANDHAR

Cover Design and Illustrations: Shayashkar Dangol

Cover Artwork: Sia Joshi

ISBN: 978-1-7635627-1-4

First Edition: 2025

 A catalogue record for this book is available from the National Library of Australia

Published by Project Baakha Productions

www.projectbaakha.com

To my dearest Maa, for making me fall in love with Newa: Baakha: (tales).

Prologue

A muse, an icon, a phenomenon, a beauty.

The word in the *tole* (town) was that there once lived a beautiful woman with black curly hair. She had brown eyes, fair skin with two black dots, one under her right eye and the another above her lips. A muse to the poet, admiration of men and women alike, she was the beauty to be adored, many men would beg their father to let them marry her. She was a portrait of beauty. She was called Rajmati.

Her beauty was much talked about, so much so that wherever she went several eyes followed her. When all eyes fall on a person, the compliments follow along with the comments, then gossips and rumours.

Everyone has their own story to tell, their own assumptions to carry and assumptions, mostly if not always, does more harm than good.

Chapter 1

The sky was in a remarkable shade of blue after a heavy downpour that cleared all the dust and submerged the pollution in the air, to the ground. The valley looked and smelt particularly beautiful after such rain- something many had thoroughly enjoyed in their existence.

"Oh, it is the rain of change," someone in the street spoke suggesting that the chilly winter was soon to arrive. Thats how people in the valley recognized that the new season was arriving. It was always the sudden rain that acted as a closing ceremony of one season and the opening of another.

It was one of those days when the rain subsided to welcome winter or to bid farewell to the summer. Amidst the recently cleared sky and smell of petrichor still lingering in the air, the beauty of the town walked through the lane clearing the road and turning heads. She had taken over hearts of most of the men in the *tole*. Breathtakingly beautiful lady with a truly

3

kind heart was something she was known for. She was wearing a black dress with long sleeves that had red borders on each sleeve and as always, she had adorned *Bizakani* over her ear. It was one of a kind piece of ear ornament. It had circular end with motif of peacock and flower that was attached to her earlobe and the chain shaped like flower petals would run from the top of the circular part in front of the ear to the back and connected as lock to the earring. She always looked gorgeous, well dressed and very much charming.

"She is the most beautiful girl in the town," one would say while the other would wave their hand around and argue, "no, no, she must be the most beautiful woman in the world." People would swarm around, talk about her like she was some sort of daily news.

She greeted her two friends, Tara and Charu, with a wave. Everywhere they went, people couldn't help but notice the trio, although it was clear that Rajmati was always the centre of attention. Among them, Tara was the tallest, with olive-toned skin, and she wore a tiny version of *Taya:* —an amulet featuring pointed ends on both sides and small snakes coming out in the centre, with a necklace bead made of red stones called *mugaa*. In contrast, Charu was fairer than Tara but similar in height to Rajmati, and her presence was easily recognized by the sound of her silver anklet *Paaya*, ringing whenever she was nearby.

"Thank you so much, both of you for helping me out with this," said Tara as soon as Rajmati reached them both.

"No problem at all. Happy to help," said Rajmati smiling, and all three of them walked towards the venue. Charu and Rajmati were helping Tara with an event she was organising for her client. Tara was a freelance event manager and

4

influencer. As she was slowly growing her work portfolio, her friends were always trying their best to help her out as best as they could. Rajmati took out the printed flyers from her bag and gave it to Tara.

Soon, Tara began engaging with the venue manager, and the three of them started working diligently on the arrangements. "Ah, it's looking wonderful, —let's hope they love it," Charu exclaimed, admiring the decoration they had managed to create together.

"I hope so," Tara added nervously.

"Of course, they would," Rajmati said reassuringly. Right then, her phone pinged with notification and after reading her message, she raised her head saying, "Guys I think I need to go. They are delivering some items today and I need to be there."

"Oh yeah yeah, you should go. We just have to wrap up things. Charu and I can do it," Tara said and turning towards Charu she added hesitantly, "right?"

Charu smiled and said, "Of course."

"A flower for an even more beautiful flower," a gentleman spoke to Rajmati, extending a single carnation towards her surprising all three of them. It was Nhugha, the florist, Rajmati was currently dating.

According to the gossip of the town, Nhugha and Rajmati had been dating each other since they were in Grade 10 and he used to bring flowers to her every day from his father's shop but if you ask Rajmati, she will say that they started dating only after completing their high school. Nhugha had very fair face and light brown eyes and worked at his father's flower shop, "Swaa: maa Florist." Because of his fair skin, he earned the nickname, *Tuyucha,* which meant fair one in Nepal Bhasa.

While many had eyes on her she was in love with one who brought her flowers every day. She kindly took that flower from his hand, smiled and put it on her hair while thanking him. Her curls were framing her face at the front and her bun was neatly made at the back and now with added carnation on the bun, it put glow in her face even more.

He smiled and said, "It looks even beautiful adorned in your hair."

"Argh! you and your cheesy line," Tara said moving her hands toward her mouth, gesturing to vomit.

"*Tuyucha*, it is time for you to bring *Lakha*: to her home, not just flower to her every day," Charu, chided him. As Rajmati and Nhugha had been dating for seven years now, her friends had been teasing him about asking her hand in marriage already. In this instance, Charu was referring to *Lakha*: which was brought to the bride side of the family from the groom side to finalise the talk of wedding and fix the date. But he never even popped the question and as usual would just smile or laugh around but never added any answer or word to her friends' teasing.

And like always he shied away from the question, so Rajmati fill the silence with, "What's the rush? We will get there when we have to." All of them nodded and engaged in some little conversation then all of them parted their ways to do their work.

Tara and Charu walked away laughing and talking to one another.

Rajmati turned towards him and said, "I am sorry, they can be-"

"It's alright, I don't mind," he interrupted shrugging his shoulders.

She nodded to that response and wondered if he ever was going to pop the question, but she was also worried that he might close off like last time when she asked him the similar question.

"Oh, I almost forgot, I got you this- your favourite. This one is made at home," she said taking out ailah from her black tote bag. Her parents made strong rice wine at home for different festivals, and she always made sure she gave a bottle to him and his family because they loved their home-made spirits.

"Oh wow, thank you so much," he exclaimed after taking the bottle and keeping it in his bag. As they were now walking on a dirt path of narrow alley surrounded by tall houses leaning against other tall houses, he asked, "Do you have to work there?" he asked.

"I don't just work there; it is something I look after just like you look after the flower shop of your dad's," she stated. It was the discussion they had had quite a few times already.

"Your father is barely there, and I don't find it safe that you are working there on your own," he replied curtly.

7

"It is fine. You know, we have to run it for now," she explained while matching his pace.

"Until when?" he asked impatiently, halting his steps in the middle and turning towards her. She also stopped and looked at him in surprise because she was not sure why he was bringing it up out of nowhere and why he seemed more annoyed this time, so she asked, "Why are you bringing this up again?"

Nhugha stayed silent and looked away without saying anything, then started walking again, the sound of the footsteps filling the silence.

"I just care about you," he added after a while, "and I am worried about you. That place is stressful. The work and everything around it."

"Well, what option do you think we have?" He went silent again as he didn't have answer to that.

"Don't worry. I am fine. Everything will be fine, alright?" she reassured.

They were now standing in front of a flower shop, Swaama: Florist, where he worked and managed the business on behalf of his father, while his father focused on the production and larger side of his business with his elder brother. They stood there for a while looking at each other, one's eyes full of concern, while another's eyes reassuring everything was going well. Then they bid each other goodbye, and she crossed the street to walk to the secret bar of the town.

Chapter 2

It is a human nature for people to peek into other people's lives or have this innate curiosity to know the secret of another person. Maybe that's why we humans are lured towards the very public life of celebrities, wanting to know what is happening in their private life, their secrets and what not. And maybe that is why people are lured into the secret bar as well—to have a chance at unveiling the secret, solving the puzzle and being part of a secret.

Another thing Rajmati was known for, apart from her beauty and kindness, was being the woman who sold alcohol—a profession often frowned upon by the upper-class society.

Located in a narrow alley of Itumbahal, beside one of the oldest bookstores that had books overflowing out of their shop, there was a wooden door carved with ancient

9

architecture. If one does not know about it, they tend to miss out its tell-tale sign that hung above the door. It was a small sized neon icon that was in the shape of *antee*- an alcohol pouring vessel that was tilted, ready to pour out the poison. No words, just that icon and inside the door that very much looked like an entrance way to any other home in that tole, held a secret bar that came alive right after clock struck six. Once you gave it a knock, it opened up to a narrow pathway that was illuminated by dim fluorescent light leading towards the bar with the glass cabinet displaying the range of alcohol as the backdrop. Above that cabinet shone in white neon light was the sign that held the bar's name- **ItumBar**- talk of the town.

Once someone entered this place, they would feel like they had travelled in past and walked into a living room of an aristocrat. There was different structural hint to highlight that. There was no billiard table or loud music. A mellow instrumental tune composed by varied artists would be playing at the background and people would be busy conversing with one another in that atmosphere. The bar had an overall speakeasy vibe as if it held secrets. The ambience was dark yet warm, mysterious of some sort. The venue in itself was like a character that one would like to learn more about that it did not require an added entertainment.

The word in the town was that the house that now held this bar used to be a place where secret meetings were held to topple governments to bring democracy in the country. Maybe that is why Rajmati wanted to keep up with the ruse by converting the previously secret junction of meetings and revolution to a secret bar.

Some days were quiet, and some days people would start swarming in as soon as the light outside the door turned neon green. There were few tables attached to the wall paired with a high stool, while there were tables strewn on the floor with normal chairs. There were also few round bar tables for the people who would like to stand with a drink and converse or look around. At the opposite end of the bar, there was an elevated structure with a concrete wall that now held a mural painting of the Kathmandu valley painted by her friend Charu. Below that painting was couple of short height tables paired with two-seater couch attached to its back wall.

If one wanted to find Rajmati, they would find her at Itumbar —the bar she now managed on behalf of her father. Ever since her father fell ill, she had taken charge of the business. No one asked her if that was what she wanted but the responsibility had been handed to her as something that was expected of her. The beauty of hers might also be one of the reasons, patrons flock to this establishment to enjoy good *ailah*.

Sitting at the far end of the venue was the popular Nepal Bhasa and Nepali language poet, Kavya Karmacharya. One of these tables was unofficially reserved for him. He always made sure to come there on Thursdays and sit in that very spot. He usually arrived a little early to see the place during its quieter hours while Rajmati was still setting up the place for the evening. She rarely had any help in the bar, as she mostly toiled away by herself.

Kavya was often alone, yet he chose a table that seated more than one person. He would order his drink at the bar, wait until it was ready, then take it back to his usual spot. The back wall that Kavya had come to adore of this place was mostly the neglected part as it was located far from the bar, thus far from the beauty behind the bar. For him, it had the perfect vantage point— this secluded corner allowed him to observe people and, hopefully, get inspiration for his work.

It offered a direct view of Rajmati at work behind the bar and also of the rest of the venue and its patrons. Though he would argue that it was the most comfortable one, he would not share this preference openly because then he might have to lose this space to others— the space, he had started to call his in this place of hers.

Such places tends to draw in writers, poets, artist alike because human nature is fascinating and when intoxicated, it shows a rather colourful side— the side that stood contrast to the venue's monotone brownish colour of the paint in the wall and that, itself, was like admiring the art. Being at such places gave artist like Kavya ideas to write. He used to go to cafes, bookshop, bars, different clubs but nowadays, this bar had been a place he frequented the most.

When slowly people started swarming into the venue, he would start his people watching. A group of college students walked in some scrolling through their phone and some snapping selfie. A couple walked in and sat on the seat attached to the wall. Then few men walked to the bar, tried flirting with women waiting for the drinks in the bar but when they failed miserably, they ordered their drinks. There were nice men, good Samaritan men, and there were sleazy men, and these men are the reason Kavya was ashamed of the gender he represented. But the girls need not have to worry because there was a huge bouncer right at the door who could see the bar and was ready to be in action if needed.

Most of the customers would always be busy flocking over around the bar where she would be serving them alcohol. They would try to woo her and fail terribly. One could wonder if the attempt was to woo her or to embarrass themselves. She would politely refuse their advancement and worked gracefully around the bar- pouring drinks, talking with her friends who also visited frequently. She seemed to enjoy doing bartending job and if there was ever a hint of sadness, she never showed it.

"I didn't know I would find you in a bar of all the places," said a burly looking man addressing Kavya. Upon hearing his voice, Kavya raised his head to find his friend looking at him questioningly. He responded, "Well, a man can wander around and get himself some poison of choice at times."

"You and your way with words. Last time I checked wanderers do not come to same place often. The word on the town is that you are quite a regular here, so much for wandering around. Are you also lining up to be her suitor or drinking over unrequited love for her?" his friend said pointing at the curly haired bartender across the room.

"I would not say I am not attracted to her; I am very much bemused by her like every other person in this bar who is here to have a glimpse of her, but I am also interested in how her beauty had enraptured so many hearts," he replied waving his hand around all the people in the bar.

Chapter 3

The dawn of change was upon the country; people wanted to try something new and make a better life for themselves. Saankhu lay on the outskirts of the valley, but Rajmati's father wanted to be at the centre of it, with plans to establish a small brewery to sell his famous "*Ailah*" in the bustling city. The alcohol he brewed had been popular in his hometown, so he decided to take a bold step of bringing the whole equipment to the capital. He uprooted the entire family from Sannkhu when Rajmati was just a child, to pursue his vision. Despite the objections from his family- his mother and the brothers, he packed up his stuff and brought his wife and daughter to the valley of opportunities.

Initially, he bought a small two storey house in Itumbahal and decided to conduct a brewing process at the back of the house while keeping local restaurant serving Newar snacks at the front and the family would live at the second storey of the house. He invested all his savings and borrowed some money

14

to make it happen. The restaurant offered snacks that paired well with alcohol—dried and spiced meats like *Sukuti*, and nuts prepared with a variety of spices, such as *Badaam Saadeko*. Occasionally, they also sold lentil pancakes known as *Baara*. While the venture required immense effort, it was managed solely by him and his wife, with occasional helping hands working for minimum wage. Over time, it became increasingly challenging to keep the business running. Though the idea was very new and exciting at that time, the idea of changing with the time came a little too late. At first, the diners were flocking to their *Newa: Khaja Ghar*, where the customers enjoyed the freshly brewed alcohol alongside delicious snacks. However, competition gradually increased as more Newar restaurants opened, offering an expanded range of dishes. They did not have enough hands to prepare more dishes, and their signature alcohol alone could not sustain them. Though people would go elsewhere for the food, they still returned for the alcohol. People would order *ailah* from them for any festivals' *nakhtya*: and occasions. However, those sales were not enough to survive the business or pay off the debt. When sustaining restaurant side of business became hard with food prices going up and gas supplies disrupted by border lockdowns, he resorted to selling only alcohol.

Slowly the rumours started spreading about the new owner of the old house. Most of the rumours held the similar underlying message- the clever businessman from Sankhu could not keep up with the demands of the city and was now drowning in debt. Was it a wishful thinking of many or the harsh reality?

During one of their dinners, Rajmati suggested an idea to her father, "Baa, as we are only selling alcohol with few inexpensive food items, how about we market it like a bar?"

"What do you mean? We are selling it like a bar. People are not coming anyway," his frustration dripping like venom as he gulped down the *ailah* in front of him.

"How about you stop drinking the alcohol with your friends that you are supposed to be selling, huh?" her mother shouted from the kitchen where she was putting the dish away.

"*Hyaa, haali mate:* - Stop Talking," her father retorted sharply. Not wanting to be part of their never-ending argument, Rajmati further suggested, "I was thinking how about we make it a secret bar?"

"Secret? People already aren't coming when they know about it. Why would they come if it's a secret?"

"People like forbidden and hidden things—things that feel exclusive or hard to find. If we advertise in—"

"Advertise? Do you think we have that kind of money to invest in advertising?" her father interjected.

"We have social media these days. I have friends in my campus who can help promote our bar, but I need to make few changes if you give me the permission," she said hurriedly.

Her father contemplated a bit on it, shook his head but didn't say anything then her mother spoke as she joined them, "Nothing is happening anyways. If it is not going to cost you any money, let her do it. Maybe it *will* generate some money to pay off debt."

Upon that her father nodded his head in affirmation and Rajmati stood up excitedly clapping her hands and said, "But

I do need to make few changes though and that might cost a little money."

Her father shook head in disappointment and said, "Well, then you need to figure out that part because I cannot really help with that."

She nodded.

She had some savings set aside for minor expenses, and for the rest, she relied on DIY solutions. She also received some help from her friends and a few supportive patrons who volunteered their time and effort. With the tactical usage of social media, the bar quickly gained popularity as one of the town's most intriguing spots. Its secretive nature piqued people's curiosity, drawing them in. However, a strong social media presence didn't always translate into significant profits—it simply meant the bar was well-known and sustaining that popularity came with its own costs.

Chapter 4

Slowly the days were getting shorter, festivities were recently over with *Bhai Tika* and *Chhath Parva* celebrated throughout the country a week ago. The wintry weather was looming in the valley with dew religiously attending leaves every morning. People could be seen layering their clothing with warm jackets, beanies and even gloves. Despite the cold, people made sure to visit their local temples in the morning greeting each other, "*Taaremaam,*" on the way. Some were rushing to catch their regular commute, rushing to work, students were fooling around walking to their schools, and some were catching up with each other stopping on the walkway sharing the local gossip while some were busy talking with shopkeeper about how things were getting expensive.

The sun was now bright in the sky- unlike summer, people were more appreciative of the warm sun these days. They wanted to sit under the sun a little moment longer holding on to the tea they bought from the nearby street vendor. Kavya was just sitting idly on one of the sitting areas also called *falcha* looking at people walking by living their mundane lives or maybe a colourful one.

"*Kabiji, Taaremam,*" an elderly man greeted Kavya addressing him by his title as *Kabi* (poet) and added Ji as a term of respect.

"Taaremam Mani Ratna Ji, *mha fu?*" Kavya replied addressing the man by his name and asking him if he was well. Mani Ratna made a gesture with hands like wave suggesting, life is going on and his crunched-up eyebrows spoke in volumes that meant, 'Well, its life, it goes on, what can we do about it. I am fine I guess.'

He then brought out *gwarmari* from the bag he was holding and offered it to Kavya asking if he would like some of those fried dough- which looked like proliferates. He thanked him and took one from the bag made out of newspaper.

"So, when can I expect the manuscript of your new poem collection?" Mani asked cutting to the chase.

Kavya looked down at the ground- the words were now failing him not only when working with papers but also in the conversation.

"I understand, words don't always come easily, that is why I have already waited for a year now. You told me you would get it done. I have already promised people with it. As your agent, I need to know the progress or at least if it is happening or not."

"It is happening," Kavya reassured.

"So how long will it take? Just give me a date," Mani Ratna insisted.

"I will give you more information around it within this month, is that ok?"

"Yes. Okay, then. Here, have some more *gwarmari*," Kavya took offered *gwarmari* and later Mani Ratna walked away leaving Kavya anxious with the self-imposed deadline.

Right then, he saw Rajmati and her friends Tara and Charu walking by laughing and talking, lost in their own world while rest of the world paused and looked at them in awe. The sound of laughter spreading like a beautiful music around the surrounding. Men stumbled on one another while trying to multitask between watching her and walking the road like a sober person.

Rajmati and her friends were carrying couple of boxes and judging from the items peeking through one of the boxes, it contained decorative items. The sound of laughter was now replaced by the sound of screech. As she passed by the *dhungedhara*, the traditional stone fountain for drinking water, the slippery sandal of Rajmati gave away on the wet ground making her lose the balance which led to landing her body harshly on the floor with her hand taking the blow and the items of the boxes strewn over the ground. Her friends quickly turned towards her and tried to help but she was quick on her feet and got up by herself laughing at the predicament. She and her friends started putting on the items that had fallen from the box. People swarmed around her asking if she was alright and if she needed help.

Kavya whose eyes had been trained on her the moment her laughter reached his ears, had stood up to go help her but the swarm of people prevented him from doing so.

He heard her thank others, "Thank you for asking. I am ok."

A moment later, she left just as she arrived and the world moved on like they would after looking at the fireworks in the sky- momentarily awed.

Itumbar had become somewhat like his temple— a shrine to visit on particular day of the week like a devout devotee. This week he could not understand his own feelings. The attraction he had for her- he could not address it. He went straight to home that evening and stayed in, though it was the night he religiously visited Itumbar.

Kavya kept on reminiscing seeing her walking down the path in the bright day light laughing with her friends. He had only seen her in the dim light of the bar, her eyes sparkling in the dark but in the daylight and even in the mess of a fall, she looked gorgeous. Then suddenly, he was very aware of his feelings for her. It was not lust, not love either but it was more of an admiration. She who seemed rather a distraction to him had now become a muse for him to write about. His next big idea and nothing more— at least that is what he told himself.

He enjoyed looking at her from afar like she was a beautiful painting made by a renowned artist, to be savoured from afar and never to approach close. He could never dream of coming close to her, but he wanted to know her story- Rajmati's story.

That night he penned a blank page that had been staring at him since past six months and the title of it was Rajmati.

Chapter 5

Itumbar was lively that night, with people walking in excitedly with their phone at their arm's length capturing their surroundings with their camera app. Some of them ordered drinks while some of them ordered light snacks. The place had been quiet for few months after initial charm of mystery slowly disappearing. The reason for quiet period could also have been because there were lots of festivals going on and people were busy drinking at their own homes than visiting bars.

"Wouldn't it be so lonely to visit bar during this time of the year?" Rajmati's father would give reasoning to her mother when she noticed how bar seemed rather empty. And he was right, as soon as the festivities had come to an end, the crowd slowly began to grow in the bar night after night.

The city people who went to countryside to celebrate were now back making the city lively all over again, the school was

22

now back on full swing and so was all the businesses with people coming back to their regular lives.

Charu and Tara visited the bar as religiously as they could and helped to promote the bar with their social media followers. That night, Tara brought along her group of friends from her social circle to show them the bar and hangout. Charu came shortly after from her 9-to-5 job and sat on the bar stool in front of the bar wall behind which Rajmati was serving her signature concoctions to the patrons.

When the customers flow reduced, they continued with their conversation that was most likely stopped in the middle previously, "So, as I was saying, my aunt came over with yet another marriage proposal for me. I am honestly so tired of this," Charu exclaimed her frustration while Rajmati shook her head in disappointment at her friend's relatives' nosiness. Tara had now joined them briefly to grab drinks and catch up with their conversation. Charu continued after sipping her cocktail, "With *Mangsir*, coming up and all the wedding invitation, my parents are like they are on some 'get-married-soon' drugs. I don't know how long I can escape this dread from being reality. I really don't want to get married. I feel like I am still young, you know."

Tara then added, "Of course we are. You have no idea how much my family wants to get rid of me. I still haven't found a way to tell them about my boyfriend." Tara then took a handful of peanuts from the small plate and put it in her mouth.

"That reminds me Rati, your parents know about you and Nhugha, aren't you two getting hitched soon?" Charu asked next looking at Rajmati who was now facing away from the bar, busy arranging the glasses at the back of the cabinet.

23

"He is not ready," Rajmati said curtly with a sigh, putting the last of the glass onto the cabinet.

Before either of her friend could respond to her statement, someone cleared their throat. Adorning his usual white shirt and khaki pant, Kavya stood waiting for them to respond.

Rajmati turned around quickly and apologized, "*Jojolapa*, Kabi ji, I am sorry I didn't see you coming in." She was well aware of his status as poet and writer, hence, Rajmati always called him by his title.

"*Jojolapa*, Rajmati ji and please, do not apologise. I only have arrived just now," he responded with a smile.

She glanced slightly towards her two friends because it was unusual for them to see him on Sunday. His regularity was so common that it became something they noticed and talked quite a lot about. Even when bar was not busy, he would be there sitting at that particular seat drinking his whiskey with a leather-bound diary placed on the table but never opened. They used to theorise that he was drafting his next big book on the people visiting this bar— which was not entirely farfetched.

"What can I get you? The usual?" she asked. Another thing one needed to know about their regular patrons was their regular choice of drink.

"The usual," he said with a smile.

He was not only particular about the day and the seating of choice but also his drink. It was always whiskey on the rocks and the days he was feeling fancy it would be the strongest *ailah* made in the house.

24

"I have to say, I am surprised to see you here on Sunday," she said to Kavya as she put his drink on the bar top.

"So, you noticed?" he tried to flirt to which Rajmati was shocked momentarily because he had never tried to flirt with her before this.

"Well, as a bar owner, I should be aware of the regular visitor," she responded back hiding her amusement.

He took the glass from its coaster and spoke before taking a sip, "I have been thinking of visiting more often than I used to."

"Well, that is great. We are happy to have you here," she said with her customer service smile and asked politely, "If you don't mind me asking, what made you make that decision."

He smiled looking at his drink and then raising his head towards her, he said, "I have been trying to write some poems for my upcoming book, but I am having hard time I am hoping that this ambience, people here would inspire me, so I come here with hopes."

"That sounds exciting. I hope you find what you are looking for here," she replied giving her rare meaningful smile, then she added, "I am sure, it will come by and take you by surprise. Persevere Kabiji. We all are looking forward to your new book."

He nodded and walked towards his usual choice of seat at the back end of the venue. He did have an intention to get an inspiration for his next write up and he *was* there to people watch. Well, it was an entirely another story that he was distracted by Rajmati most of the time he was there, and she had now become his muse. He wanted to write about her instead of another anthology of poems about humans and society.

"Gosh, it such a privilege, isn't it? To be able to pursue your passion. To be able to afford your dreams," Charu said turning to look at the poet walking away with his drink on his hand.

"What are you talking about?" Tara asked looking at her phone.

"About Kavya, the Kabi. If I tell my parents I want to pursue painting and do exhibitions, would they let me?" Charu scoffed returning to her drink and gulping it down in one go.

"Yeah, you are right. It is indeed a privilege," Rajmati sighed picking up the bottle and moved away to put some bottles back to the cabinet. She stayed there looking at the glass cabinet full of bottles with alcohol trapped inside them. She wondered if she was also trapped in this place.

"Gosh, but Kavya is really cute, huh?" Charu expressed looking longingly at the poet who was now scribbling in his diary that he finally opened in this place. Charu's words breaking the trance that Rajmati was in and making her turn towards Charu in surprise.

"That was so random," Tara said and began teasing her, "oohh, do you have a crush on him?"

"Wow, really?" Rajmati added, "Shall I introduce you to him?"

26

Charu nodded and then blushed before adding, "You know, actually, I have not told you guys, I had a crush on him ever since I read one of his poems. Then I saw him coming here and I have been dying to talk to him."

"Then, go and talk to him," Tara encouraged.

"No, I don't think I can," Charu hesitated.

"It so makes sense as well. Artist falling for another artist," Tara continued teasing Charu.

"Delivery from Swaamaa: Florists for the beautiful Rajmati," Nhugha's voice interrupted them, and they stopped their conversation right there.

Rajmati blushed at the gesture of her boyfriend, who was now on his knees bestowing her the set of beautiful bouquet of flowers. She took it from his hand and in return went to bar and gave him the small shot glass filled to the brim with patron he loved so much. He took the shot and started talking to her about his day while Kavya looked attentively at their interactions.

The way his hand moved towards her face, the way he played with her curls while Tara teased them both, "Gosh! You two get a room."

"*Tuyucha*, why don't you bring some flowers to us as well time to time," Charu added next.

"Why should I get you one? You are not my girlfriend," he retorted back as usual. For some reason, Charu and Nhugha never got along since their school days. They always come out at each other with their sharp words for each other. Their banter began and lasted for a minute then Charu huffed and walked away from the bar taking Tara with her.

"You two can never stop arguing, can you? Gosh!" Rajmati shook her head in disappointment.

Nhugha then laughed and turned towards her asking, "Are you free tomorrow afternoon?"

"Yes, why do you ask?"

"Let's go on a brunch date, it has been a while," he said resting his hand over the bar top.

"Don't you have a shop to run?"

After his college, he had been given sole responsibility to look after it just around the same time Rajmati converted the bar theme. However, both of them were already helping their parents in their work frequently when they were in school. Swaamaa: Florist was right opposite the bar so they would see each other quite often as well even when they were not dating. Their friendship bloomed from their frequent encounter near the shops and them going to same school. But unlike Itumbar, Swaamaa was flourishing because flowers were needed on every occasion.

"We have got a part-time staff to look after the shop while I am not there," Nhugha said. He had been trying to convince Rajmati to hire a part time help at the bar so that she can rest time and again. However, she couldn't yet afford a new permanent staff due to some outstanding debts to vendors and a loan that her family was struggling to pay off.

Rajmati had wanted to hire someone new for quite a while now but the fluctuating crowd at the bar made it hard for her to feel confident about committing to additional wages. She had a couple of workers she could call occasionally, but with the bar's uncertain situation, she hadn't been able to give them consistent hours, and as a result they had taken jobs elsewhere.

She was planning on sorting out some bills for the venue next day, but it had been a while since she and Nhugha went out together, so she agreed to go out with him for the brunch.

"Sounds good," she said with a smile.

"Great, I will pick you up," he chimed.

Next day, however, only his text arrived, "I am sorry, babe, I can't make it. Mom wants me to do some errand for her. I will see you in the *Thecho Jatra*." She was however disappointed that he couldn't make time for yet again.

Chapter 6

"Yomari Chwaamu! U ke dune Hwaamu!"

Almost every full moon day comes with an occasion in Kathmandu valley. In the chilly full moon day of winter, families gather around, make *Yomari,* and share it with their neighbours. Yomari is one of the favourite delicacies of the people living in the valley- the name Yomari's literal translation is 'favourite delicacy.' It made from rice flour dough which is turned in a cone like or fig-like shape then filled with liquid dark molasses also known as *Chaaku;* the filling also consists of sesame seeds. It is then steamed and eaten warm. *Chaaku* would spill through after a bite or two, the hot molasses burning the mouth but warming the heart and if you are not careful enough it might ruin your favourite shirt. All the family members come together and start making this dish from the morning. After it is done, they would put some of it aside as offerings for the Gods and Goddesses while the rest is shared among family members and little children who come outside houses humbly chanting:

"Yomari Chwaamu! U Ke dune Hwaamu,
Biu sa lyasse, Mabiusa Budi Kuti!!"
Yomari is yummy! full of sesame,
If you give it to me, you're a beautiful young lady,
If you do not give it to me, you are stingy old lady!!

While it is a day of giving and sharing, it is also a day when young lovers ask their crush out on a date for the next day. under the guise of visiting houses to ask for Yomari, would also ask their crush out for a date the next day. During the time when people did not have the privilege of technology like today, it is said that on the occasion of *Yomari: Punhi*, men would visit the house of their lover under the guise to ask for *Yomari* and also ask them out for a date; fix the time and location of where they would meet. Therefore, the day after the *Yomari Punhi* is called *Matina Paru,* the day to celebrate love. Some people still followed this tradition asking their beloved on a date to go out on Matina Paru.

The bar was closed that day because they were making Yomari at home. It was mostly three of them, Rajmati and her parents. Sometimes they would go to Saankhu to visit family but in recent years, visits were reduced to only major festivals. She had told her mother that after making Yomari she was planning to go out with Nhugha for a moment to see *Thecho Jatra*, which was a celebratory procession that happened in Thecho during *Yomari Punhi*.

"So, are you two only going to roam around or are you also planning to get married as well, huh?" her mother asked sarcastically.

Rajmati's mother has been pressuring her to get married with Nhugha because she would rather see them married than just dating one another. As most people had known of their relationship, her mother did not want the people to talk about them and how they were not married but fooling around.

"People will start talking, you know, who knows they already have," her mother continued as Rajmati continued kneading the dough in silence with no intention to respond. Her mother poured the rock of *Chaaku* on to the pan making it sizzle then turned towards her, "If you both are sure of spending life with each other then what is stopping you. I don't understand what is going on here. If you do not talk to him then I will talk to a matchmaker, I am telling you."

"I don't know Maa. I think he is talking to his parents," she finally spoke.

"I don't think he is. As you are meeting him today, ask him what is going on here. Time does not wait for everyone my dearest," her mother said sternly with concern in her eyes.

"Well, I don't want to talk about it anymore," Rajmati replied.

"Ok, if you say so," her mother said looking at the melting *Chaaku* in the stove. Both mother and daughter worked silently making the cone shape out of the dough and filling in with gooey *Chaaku*, then closing them up by making little horns at top.

After a moment, her mother got up from her seat and put all the Yomari in the steamer and walked towards the window to check outside if Rajmati's father had arrived from the store but instead she saw someone else parking their motorbike.

"Your boyfriend is out there, waiting for you with flower in hand as usual so you should go. Your father and I will wrap things up here once he is back from store. Come home early so that we can at least spend this day together as a family."

Rajmati checked her phone and saw that he had sent a text message regarding his arrival just a minute ago.

Rajmati looked up at her mother and sighed.

"I'll try to talk to him today, alright?" she told her mother, and her mother simply nodded.

"Wait, Yomari is going to be ready so ask him to wait for a moment and take it with you," her mother said.

Nhugha smiled as he looked at her and gave her the bunch of peonies, all in the colour pink, while she gave him the Yomari. She blushed as she took peonies from him. He had been bringing her flowers ever since they met but every time it made her blush like it did the first time.

***

It was sunny day, and children were roaming around the school grounds. Some were running touching the tree saving themselves from the Tag game, which allowed them to escape from tag as long as they touched the tree, some students were sitting in nearby benches and sharing lunch while some were busy ordering Mo: Mo: from the only canteen that served the dish in the school.

"*Swaa yah laa?* Do you like flowers?" he teased her bringing a lone pair of dandelions towards her. The very first flower Nhugha brought for Rajmati. She was sitting on the steps of the playground in her school uniform when he joined her. She took it from him and blew on it making all the white particles to fly away. She giggled as the white flurry fill the air.

"You were supposed to make a wish first," he said.

"Maybe I did make a wish," she added.

"What did you wish for?" he asked.

"You don't tell people what you wish for," she retorted.

"Can I tell you something?" he asked next.

"Sure."

"I like you," he confessed.

She was surprised at first, then she smiled and nodded without saying anything.

"You must hear that a lot, I know. You are the most beautiful girl in the school- maybe in the world. But you know what, I can make you happy. I can always make you smile, and I will always bring you flowers to make your day. I want to marry you someday."

She brought her both hands to her mouth when he said that last line. She had smiled then and didn't reply anything on that day. The bell rang and all of them rushed to the class.

Next week, he again had brought flowers, this time it was the flower that would last better than the dandelions. It was red roses and when he handed it to her, he told her that he is immensely enamoured by her. It was not something she hadn't heard enough already from other boys of her age. She was the popular girl in school and there were young boys falling for her, saying beautiful things to her but for some reason Nhugha had stolen her heart. His words felt sincere than the most, so after months and months of contemplation and finishing their high school, she had finally told him that she liked him too. He had promised her then, "I will always make you smile. I will give you all the happiness."

Seven years since the first time they confessed love for each other and many things had changed ever since. There were rainy days, sunny days, and also cold harsh winter but rarely days of spring in their love life and mostly autumn now. Autumn because it felt like a transitional period, beautiful but with anticipation of frigid winter. It was one long autumn for them.

***

They had promised each other to go to Thecho Jatra on Yamari Punhi, and despite their busy schedules, they made it happen. They bought Mo: Mo: from a street vendor who was selling warm foods. Carrying a bowl made out of dried leaves, filled with steaming Mo: Mo:, they sat in a nearby seating area to enjoy an unobstructed view of the Jatra.

Rajmati decided to bring out the Yomari her mother had thoughtfully packed in an insulated bag. She took one out and gave it to Nhugha and then took another one out for herself. They both blew on it to cool the hot fillings and took a bite as chaku slightly oozed from the bread. When a bit of chaku fell on his cheek, she instinctively moved toward him to wipe it off. However, before she could reach him, he moved away and wiped it off himself, looking away. She was momentarily puzzled by his action but chose not to say anything and turned her gaze away.

Slowly the music started filling the air and the procession started. They were now standing to see the procession more properly and in the entirety of Jatra, their eyes roamed everywhere but rarely at each other. looked at the Jatra and rarely at each other.

After some time, Rajmati noticed that Nhugha was lost somewhere this time unlike other times when he would be lost in his phone. He was now looking at her time and again as if he was trying to conjure up some words to speak but failing each time. Rajmati couldn't handle the awkwardness of silence and his loss of words, so she spoke up first, "Is there something bothering you?"

"Umm…" was the only sound that came out of his mouth then shook his head no, then looked at his phone, scrolling through the content but never paying attention. One could hear Dhime Baja playing from afar and by the sound of it, it was approaching them soon.

"Can we talk?" she asked.

"About what?" he questioned back. A sacred masked dances were happening on the street while two of them were looking at each other in an intense gaze.

"About anything. How about how was your day? Mine was good thank you. How about you? We have barely talked in past few weeks. Do you have nothing to talk to me about?" she blurted out to him. In the heat of the moment, she blurted out everything but not the thing she wanted to ask which was, *'Are we drifting away? Why is this silence awkward all of a sudden? Why did you look at him like you want to tell me something but look away?'*

36

"It's not like that. We have always been comfortable like this. We don't have to talk about every silly thing. There is a Jatra going on, the noise is so loud, we can barely hear each other anyways." To that she pulled him by his hand and took him to the alley nearby.

"Ok, what do you *really* want to talk about?" he asked sneakily leaning towards her and planting a kiss on her shoulder. She moved away and faced him.

He then looked at her and spoke, "Listen, you want to talk, let's talk. I just don't have anything to talk about, alright?"

"Why not? We rarely meet; we rarely talk these days. What's going on? Even if we meet, you are always on your phone. Tomorrow is Matina Paru, how about asking me out on a date for instance," she said.

"We are on a date, right now," he said with frustration.

"My world starts with you and finishes in you, and I would not have any issue with that fact, if your world also started with me and finished in mine," she said with her voice breaking slightly.

Nhugha went silent and stood there in the narrow alley with Rajmati facing him with questions he did not know how to answer to.

He remembered his recent conversation with his mother, "I have heard so many rumours about that girl. She sells ailah for God's sake. We can't have such girl as a family. I can't have her as my daughter-in-law. You cannot marry her."

"But I love her," he pleaded.

"Oh, come on, love. Love is a mere word. Do you think I loved your dad when I married him. You will learn to love your wife, and she would be the one we choose not the random alcohol selling girl. She might be beautiful, but beauty does not mean standard. Do you understand?"

When he didn't say anything, she held him by his arms and added, "You have to swear on me that you won't marry her."

"Will you say something?" Rajmati asked pulling him out of his reverie.

He looked down at the ground rather guiltily and whispered, "I can't do this anymore." Not hearing what he said amidst the soaring excitement of Jatra around them, she moved closer asking what he had said. He then took a long breath and looked up in the sky then at her. Holding her by the arms, he said, "Please forgive me. I haven't been entirely honest with you."

"What? Why are you saying that?" she asked confused.

"I talked with my parents about us." He added.

The roaring sound of Dhime came through the crowd followed by melody of flute mixing through the air. Everyone around them looked excited with their camera out to take videos and photos. The social media was going to be filled with red and gold pictures of Jatra that day.

Hearing what he had said and the excitement of Jatra around her, she smiled assuming he had finally taken the initiative of mentioning their relationship to his parents and excitedly asked, "You did? Then why didn't you say something? What did they say?"

"They…they- ahem," he cleared his throat but the sound and noise around them were louder. He looked around them and spoke, "they don't want me to see you anymore."

"What? I couldn't hear you. Let's go somewhere quieter," she spoke, and they went further into the alley where the ongoing celebration and its sound were rather faint.

"So, what did they say?" she asked curiously.

"My parents want me to get married but not with you," he said looking away from her- trying hard not to look at her at any cost.

"What- What does it mean for us?" she stuttered as she remembered the first time they met in their school.

Amidst the same crowd were now young Rajmati and Nhugha. They had been classmates since they were in grade 1. They had paired up in different group dances of the school, he had brought flowers to her almost every day even when she had not reciprocated his feelings and even more after she expressed her feelings for him. "I can always make you smile, and I will always bring you flowers to make your day. I want to marry you someday." His promise resonated in her ears while his eyes held emptiness.

Now as they face each other, Rajmati found it rather ironic that the person who promised to make her smile was the reason for her tears that she just couldn't stop. He didn't even try to wipe away her tears.

"Are you breaking up with me?" she mustered to ask.

He didn't muster enough to say anything. He just nodded.

"We can't be together anymore, Rati," he blurted it out. Those few words made her feel like she was doing a freefall from a building with no harness. She moved a step back from him and thinking she might not have understood what he had said, she spoke again, "What do you mean?"

"They have found someone else for me and want me to go meet her instead."

"But *we* are together. How will you go and see another girl. Did you tell them about me? Why are they against us? Did you tell them that you wouldn't go see them, did you-" he held her hands and she went quiet because she saw it in his face that he was giving up- that he had already decided what he was going to do.

"Is that why you were being so distant from me lately? Did you even try to fight for us?" she whispered. He didn't say anything and just looked away.

He took a deep breath and spoke, "I am sorry, Rati. You know what my family is like, and they want me to marry someone-"

"Someone who does not make ailah or serves it in a bar. Did I get that right?" Rajmati interrupted him and he did not disagree, so she continued, "Did you even defend me? Is that why you have been telling me to stop working there? It was not out of concern, was it?"

With his silence as confirmation, she stormed out of that alley. The beautiful melody of Jatra, starting to feel like a noise to her. All the memories now tainted.

40

She wiped her tears away as she walked past the swarm of people moving towards the Jatra while she was walking away from it. To be broken up the day before Matina Paru; to be told that he would marry someone else. How cruel of him to crumble her world down on her favourite day of the year. How heartless of him to wait for her to question him, instead of confessing the truth himself.

People say that love will finds its way. However, it also depends on the courage and one's willingness to walk that path and fight for their love. In the darkness, ability to find the light. Most importantly, patience to find a way.

"I have got a wonderful proposal for our Rajmati."

Chapter 7

Sleazy men, nice men, good men, all swarming around the bar like a honeybee around a flower, asking for the potion to live a little, to forget about a world a little. The bar opened during the time when people did not want to go home yet but want to leave their workstation fast. A beautiful transitional place— like a purgatory and she their host while they wait.

As always Rajmati was pouring the mixture of alcohol to some, pure spirit to someone who asked for it and water to one who clearly needed it. There were some women, swarmed around in a corner seat like beautiful flock of birds, seating closely next to each other, so that no men would mistake them to be available and make any unsavoury move. They were giggling and gossiping but not too much as to garner unwanted attention.

Drinking in all this scene along with his regular poison was Kavya, sitting at his regular seat, at the back of the venue with

42

all the view and the story unfolding. Though his intention was to look at all the patrons and get a glimpse of life in between sobriety and insobriety, he would always find himself lost looking at the bartender at the other end, working her way through the crowd and making drinks like a well-choreographed scene. There was something attractive about the way she smiled, talked to people, and listened to them— mundane things yet so attention grabbing.

It had been almost a month since he last visited as he was mostly busy travelling around the country and probably that is why he felt like a lot had changed- especially the charm of the host. He had seen her twice before his travels, first was rather coincidentally in a different setting from a bar. She seemed rather sad that day.

He wondered if she was still heartbroken over her ex-lover or something else had happened during his absence because she seemed lost. Her body was there but mind elsewhere. She had dropped a glass or two. It was a good thing that there was a new staff helping around. She smiled and talked with customers but rarely her smile met her eyes. *Or has it always been like that?* Kavya got lost in thought again, he had never seen her smile brightening her eyes. He had never seen her genuinely happy. For someone with such a beautiful smile, she seemed like someone who had never felt that smile even if it was part of hers. He decided that he would go and talk to her later and continued looking around absorbing the rest of the scene unfolding.

He was jotting down some lines in his tattered diary that he carried with him wherever he went. He felt closer to his ideas when he wrote them down. It was also a special diary not just with memories etched into it but the way he bought it as well.

The day he bought it was also the day he saw her for the first time. It was the bookshop beside Itumbar where he was looking to buy some books when his eyes fell on the very diary. Then he heard someone call her name, "Rajmati." He had heard that name quiet often in the streets when people would talk about her but never had a chance to see the beauty beholding the name. She was almost like a myth to him. When his eyes landed on her, it stayed on her, capturing his attention; he did not even realise he had added that diary in the pile of books he was buying. Since that day he had carried that diary with him like it was a souvenir from her.

As he was about to add another line from his reverie, a voice snapped him out of the world he was creating in his pages.

"Kabiji, how have you been?" asked Charu, Rajmati's friend as she approached his table with his drink. He smiled at her and was surprised to see her bringing him his drink. He looked at her and looked at Rajmati who seemed busy in the bar talking with someone.

"I have been well. How about you?" he turned his attention back to Charu and took the drink from her hand but not before thanking her.

He then added, "I didn't know you started working here," to which she chuckled a little and added, "Oh no, no, I do not work here but I am helping out, Rati today."

"That is very nice of you," he said then paused and said, "I am sorry, but I did not order this. I usually get my drink myself and I already have one here."

Charu blushed a little and said, "I know. It is from me."

He did not know what to say for a moment and slowly replied, "Thank you."

"I am sorry, I am Charu, and I am a huge fan of your books, and I just love the way you write— it is so beautiful. I always see you here, but I never got a chance to talk to you, so I just wanted to come and say hi to you," Charu blabbered nervously.

"Oh, please don't say sorry. I appreciate it, truly. It always warms my heart when someone talks so nicely of my work," Kavya smiled warmly.

"Keep up the good work, we are excited for your next book," she said smiling.

"Wait now, did my agent put you up for this because I have been pushing the deadline?" he asked jokingly and both laughed.

"Oh no! Was it that obvious?" Charu joked back and making each other laugh again. Suddenly, a broken glass shattered behind the bar.

"Ok, enjoy your drink. It was lovely talking to you. I better get going," she said.

"Sure, I am glad you came to talk to me and thank you for the drink," he said making her blush and as she was moving away, he called her, "Charu, you are a very good friend." She then nodded with a smile and rushed away with her anklet making beautiful sound with each of her steps.

***

Next week, sitting on his usual place, Kavya noticed that there was a new stranger in the bar- he had short well-maintained black hair and dusky skin and was wearing a suit. This new stranger seemed unable to get his eyes away from the one pouring another set of alcohol to a persistent customer. When she finally looked at him, he smiled at her, and she smiled back. Her smile suggested that she knew him because it was not the smile you give to the customer but to someone you had known for a long time. However, her smile also seemed full of shyness and slight awkwardness. Kavya had never seen that version of her smile. It was simply different. The stranger then walked towards her and sat opposite to the bar wall and started conversing with her making Kavya rather curious about the whole scene in front of him. At this point, he regretted choosing the last seat in the bar because he would rather listen in to the conversation than just observing the scene without sound. He wondered what that stranger could be saying that enraptured her attention.

Chapter 8

"Rajmati is getting married, did you hear?"

"Yes, I did. I heard that the matchmaker messed up."

"I wondered who would have decided to marry her. Poor girl."

"Well, she works at a bar. Who cares if she owns it, it is a bar at the end. No good family want to get married to that family."

"Seriously? At this age and time?"

"Oof, you, young people wouldn't know. Society is above everything."

"Didn't you see the guy she used to roam around with got married to someone else."

"Well, I heard the guy she is going to marry is very rich."

"I wonder why they are rushing the marriage. I mean the talk of marriage had only started and they are now getting married."

"Maybe he needed a trophy wife you know, arm candy because I heard he is rich rich."

"Maybe her family needed money to sort out their debt, who knows."

"The man will sleep around while have this wife as a show for society."

"But I heard the groom's family was not that well to do. I don't think he is that rich."

"Yeah, I heard it too, that they are poor. Maybe they are deceiving the poor girl."

"Pretty girl does not equate pretty life, I guess."

Gossips were running wild around the tole ever since the wedding invitation had been circulated. Noone had seen the groom, but the assumptions were all over the place. Kavya, however had seen him, though he couldn't converse with him properly that night at Itumbar. Roman seemed nice but what could he know from the first meeting. Kavya kept on hearing different talks around the street and some of the gossips even reached his own home. Among the gossip he would also hear bitter words like,

"I heard money was short in the house so they let her get married to a rich guy who would invest in their household as well."

"Poor girl, I heard the house she got married is not even a house."

"Rich does not mean happy life. He lives in an apartment while selling different houses."

He had heard so much of these gossips since she got married, that he started to believe some of it and naturally his

48

concern for her built. He had attended the wedding party, where she looked beautiful, normal- well, as beautifully normal as bride can look. The wedding affair was quiet and rushed. Even after a year since her wedding, he couldn't completely dismiss the chatter of the town. Maybe that is why all he could remember from that reception party of her wedding was her sadness and helplessness. It almost felt like she was putting on a façade or was it something he thought he saw?

After her wedding, he rarely saw her. Her visit to bar was getting less frequent with new bar staff being hired. She looked more relaxed around the bar whenever she visited, and they would converse a little but soon enough his visit to bar became minimal to none when he got himself engrossed in his new book. He was also getting pressure from his family to get married, but he was persistent on not marrying anyone yet – not until he found that someone himself.

***

Even after a year of marriage, there were still whispers of her married life. It was rarely a pleasant thing and mostly it was pitiful. No one knew if those rumours held any light to the truth, but people would gossip regardless. Men, women alike seemed to be interested in her marriage and in the name of being empathetic, they could only focus on how she couldn't get her happy ending, how she was not as lucky as she was beautiful. She no longer lived in the same tole, therefore, people had little to no information on how she lived. They would recycle their old gossips and reinvent new stories out of it- no one knew how much of it was myth and how much of it was real.

Despite living in a different part of the city and being married to an established businessman, people in the society

49

still found a way to ridicule the people living in it. Whenever someone mentioned her name or talk about her thriving bar in the tole, one would hear comments like,

"He didn't even take her on honeymoon."

"She does not even work at bar anymore. Somebody else does."

"Did they sell off that bar?"

"No, no they still own the place."

Their jealousy coming out in all shades of green.

"You know her husband does not even have a proper house. It is an apartment. I mean he owns the building but who wants to live in an apartment with no *Sajhya* or proper balcony with a view or a terrace to have *nakhtya* and *bhwoya*. - you know all those family functions and gatherings."

"You know one day I will live in a house away from this hustle and bustle of city with house that has got Sajhya, garden and wide balcony to look at the valley," Kavya had heard Rajmati talk about it with her friends in the past. During that conversation, one of her friends had responded, "I hope you get that house one day. Maybe you will be married into one house like that."

"I don't think I will ever marry or if I marry, I don't need my husband's house to be like that, I will rather make such house myself one day," she then giggled and took the glasses away from the bar table.

He would reminisce these conversations he had overheard at times and sometimes would just remember her fondly working at the end of the bar flaunting her curls. Some moments he would also remember their conversations and

50

how thoughtful they were. He was grateful that she had allowed him to write about her- to make her his muse in his next book.

***

It was little over a year since her wedding and probably few months since he had seen her last. When he reached her new home, he realised that the house may not have *sajhya*: or huge balcony but it certainly was big and lavish. The penthouse where she was currently living with her husband had her mark on it everywhere. Every corner of the place reflected her in some ways except for the huge picture of her and her husband. Because he knew that she had always preferred small frames of picture as opposed to the large frames of magnanimous images- or at least that was what he thought she would prefer.

"*Jojolapa* Kabiji, how are you doing? It is so nice to see you," Rajmati spoke while walking down the spiral staircase. Her hair was tied in a bun with few loose strands framing her face. She had worn her eyeliner like always with small streak curved upwards. She was glowing. If there was an elderly woman in the room seeing her after long time she would have said, "marriage suits her." But it was only Kabiji and he, the master of words, was spellbound looking at her as she stepped down to the floor. He didn't know if he was happy to see her after long time or she always had such a glow. He also was not sure if she was happy to see him or simply happy in general or if she was pretending to be happy. He could not even dare to question it.

He cleared his throat to answer her question, his words almost failing him. He brought his thoughts together and spoke, "It is so good to see you. You are just as beautiful as always if not more. How are you?"

51

She waved her hands brushing his compliment away and said, "Oh no, not at all. Gone are those youthful days. Please have a seat. I am sorry to have you come all the way here for this."

"No, it is not a problem at all." he said and proceeded to sit on the couch in front of him.

As if realising something, she brought her hand to her forehead and said, "Oh how silly of me. Let me get you some tea first."

"Oh, no please don't bother," he said courteously.

"Oh please, it would not take a moment," she said and disappeared into the kitchen.

A few moments later, she came back with a tray full of snacks and two cups of milk tea. The tray had some chocolate covered biscuits and some cakes with tiny coconut flakes around it. She put it in the table and brought a cup of tea, a small plate with biscuits and cake in front of him.

"Wow, these taste good," Kavya said taking a bite from what looked like a small slice of cake.

"I think they are called Lamington," she responded, "we brought it from our recent visit to Sydney. I love it so much, so we had to bring some of these homes and these biscuits called Tim Tam- our nieces and nephews love them."

"Yeah, it goes well with our tea," he replied.

She took a sip from her tea and bringing her palms together, she said, "It is so exciting that your book is now coming out. Congratulations!! I am so happy for you."

He brought his hand around his neck nervously thanking her, "It is all because of you to be honest. Thank you so much. I have brought the manuscript for you to read. If you find anything that is not to your liking, please let me know. I will make the changes."

She waved her hand around and said, "Oh, there is no need. You are its owner. I am merely a muse like you mentioned. Who am I to judge the work of an artist? I would not want to taint it with my opinions. Please do what you think is right. I trust you and I believe you have put all your beautiful words in action here."

"I am flattered. It would be published as a book of poetry with a ballad dedicated to you," he took a manuscript from his bag and gave it to her, "I would still love for you to have this copy."

Rajmati seemed surprised to see her name as a title page in the book full of poetry about all the lovely things. She didn't say a word and just looked at him with appreciation and tears that almost fell from her eyes.

"It should be me who is flattered with this and honestly I am. Thank you for making me part of this."

Kavya was mesmerised but he was also unsure how she would take the poetry if she read it. It did compliment her beauty but not so much about her fate. And some part of him was glad that she was not going to read it while some part of him hoped she read and told him how wrong he was.

He then asked her, "Are you happy?" catching her off guard by such question. She seemed like she did not quite understand the question let alone the suddenness of it. In response she nodded and said, "Yes, I am. Thank you for asking."

He was pleased to hear her say but he was still not sure if it was entirely a truth. He noticed that her smile was different than what he was used to seeing. It was sincere and brightened her eyes, but he had heard all these things in the tole, so his mind was convoluted for obvious reasons. He also couldn't tell if she was happy because of the book, or if she was *really* happy in her marriage. He also wondered why on such beautiful day that her husband had chosen to go outside instead of spending time with his wife.

He had written all about how beautiful she was and how unfair her fate was for so long that he did not know if he should believe her words or his words on the book he had written. He decided to not dwell on any of this longer than necessary, so he decided to bid goodbye. Before he could go, he realised he also had something else that belonged to her and decided to give it to her.

He then went ahead to take it out of his pocket. He had found it on the day he had talked to Rajmati about the book for the first time. She had already left by the time he had found it, so he had kept that as keepsake of hers. He decided that he should part with it now that the book was done, and he had no more excuses of not seeing her enough for not to return it. When he extended his hand to give it to her, she refused and said, "It's alright, I do not want it. I want things from my past to remain in past. If you don't mind, please keep it as a thank you for naming a book after me. You can give it away if you prefer."

He hesitated a little, but she insisted.

"I would rather keep it as keepsake from you to remind me of you," Kavya said with a warm smile. *He would later hang it on a hanging lamp near his bedroom window.*

Chapter 9

Rajmati looked at the manuscript he had left behind, but she could not bring herself to look into it. So, she left in the table and walked away. He must have written about the girl he had met back then, she thought, and she was nervous to open those pages. She didn't want to read it— not yet.

Soon her mind travelled back to the time when her life changed.

***

"I cannot believe your father's ego to be honest. His brother is willing to help but no, he just wants to do it by himself," Rajmati's mother was going on about how troubling the situation was getting with their Mill not doing well and the business not going well either. She was splitting beans on the terrace of their home while Rajmati was leaning against the wall pretending to listen to her mom while staring at oblivion holding one strand of green bean.

"He just does not get it. We need to marry you off as well. How are we going to get the money? A daughter's wedding is so expensive," her mother continued, now moving on to separating and tearing apart leafy greens to cook later.

The word wedding seemed to have caught Rajmati's attention, breaking her trance, so she spoke, "What if I don't get married at all? Wouldn't that be helpful for everyone?"

To that her mother looked aghast as if she had almost confessed to a crime.

"And have a spinster at home? You are on a merry way to be one anyways," she said looking at her daughter in pure dismay.

"What? I am still young," Rajmati responded back.

"Well, you won't be after some time. I am saying this for your own good. You need a partner in life. Not because you are a woman but as a person. One needs to have someone to share this life with, regardless of being a man or a woman. A person needs a life partner."

"Well, it is my life, and I have decided I don't want one. I don't want to get married," she replied angrily.

"Why? Because you thought that Tuyucha was your everything. Look at him now. He will also soon marry off some girl while he fooled around with you all this time. I have already asked *Nini* to look for a good husband for you."

Nini was the term used to address one's father's sister. Most of the matchmaker were women and usually knew most of the people in the society and would refer the patriarch of the family as *Dai*, also the word used for brother, therefore, inadvertently became Nini to their kids. However, the correct term for matchmaker regardless of their gender would have been *Lami*.

"What?" Rajmati said her voice almost loud.

It had not even been a day since her breakup and her mother was rushing to find a guy for her.

"Yes, and it is better for us to find a man for you. In that way we can ensure you have got a good partner."

Before she could say something, a middle-aged woman came up to their terrace saying, "Jojolapa, *Tataju*, are you doing well? The door was open, so I came up directly hearing your voice. And Rajmati, how are you doing?" Tataju was a term that people used to address their elder sister-in-law or as a respectful term to a married woman at certain age.

"Jojolapa *Nini*, sorry I have to go to shop to get things for the bar. See you later," she smiled and left. It was in fact just an excuse for her to leave the conversation between them.

When Rajmati was moving towards the door, she heard Nini speaking to her mother, "I have got a very good marriage proposal for our daughter. They are from a good family, trust me."

***

She rushed out of the house in hurry to avoid the talk of marriage and family. It was becoming too much for her. She let her feet finds its own way and realised she was walking towards the *dhunghedhara* near her house. She ended up looking

58

at the people coming to fill in the water from the ever-flowing water from the spout of stone faucet- *dhungedhara*. It was a mundane routine of people getting in the line to fill up the water, they put the bucket under flowing water, waits until it overflows and leaves, then the new empty bucket is being brought to fill another bucket of water. She was lost in the moment looking at these ongoing activities when she heard someone talking to her.

"Well, what a pleasant surprise to see you here today, Rajmati Ji." It was Kavya adorned in his usual white shirt and beige pant. He was wearing sunglasses this time. She had never seen him worn one before. Probably because she had only seen him inside her dim lit bar.

"Good to see you outside of the bar. I thought that was your favourite place. Is this one of the other places you frequent?" Rajmati teased him.

"I am a writer. Places like these are my workplace," he joked moving his hand to wave at passerby who smiled and waved back.

After a moment, Kavya broke the silence, "Are you waiting for someone?"

"Nope, I am just here by myself," she said looking at the people passing by.

"I thought you would be on a date today- given that today is Matina Paru," he said looking at her.

She then looked back at him and said, "Well, for that to happen, he needs to ask me out on a date during *Yomari: Punhi*, right?"

59

"As I have heard, yes," Kavya replied innocently.

"Well, he didn't... and he never will," she stated as if coming to realisation all over again. Kavya remained stunned. She looked away again before her eyes betrayed her.

"Umm I..." Kavya fumbled not knowing what to say next.

"It's alright. It was broken long time ago in a sense. We... I didn't realise that we were trying to hold onto a loose thread that had no chance of holding us together," she said. For some reason, it was easy to tell a stranger about what she thought went wrong in her relationship, but then again Kavya was not truly a stranger, and neither was he a friend. Acquaintance maybe—she did not know if it was wise of her to blurt out her thoughts to a mere acquaintance but at that moment, she did not want to be practical or understanding or pretend to know how the world worked.

He nodded in understanding. They again fell back to silence- rather awkward one this time.

She was about to leave when Kavya stopped her.

"Rajmati Ji, can I ask you something?"

Confused she responded, "Yes, sure."

He spoke, "This might sound like a strange request, but I was hoping to ask you a question lately."

"Umm...sure, please go ahead," she said.

"Your beauty is the talk of the town, surely you are aware of it, and frequenting Itumbar has become my source of inspiration, and you have sort of become my muse."

"Are you flirting with me?" she asked in confusion.

"No, not at all."

"Oh, I am glad, I got confused for a moment there. My apologies. I just am not in the right headspace, right now."

"I had been wanting to ask this question from a long time ago," he blurted out.

"And you are saying it today, because?" she asked impatiently, unsure where he was going with this. She did not have time for rebound or people flirting with her just because she had broken up with her boyfriend and even if the relationship was slowly dying a long time ago, the death of it was still recent and wound was fresh.

"Honestly, it is just the timing of me seeing you here. I understand and I would not try to flirt or win you over especially when you have just broken up. Another reason I would not do so is because I am aware of one thing that most of the men in awe of you, are not," he said.

"That is?" she asked rather curiously. Suddenly a small girl came in front of them asking if they would like a warm tea that she was selling. Rajmati and Kavya both nodded and bought tea from her. The girl thanked them and moved away with a smile.

Kavya then turned his gaze towards Rajmati and looking at her eyes, he said, "That is most of us if not all, are in love with the idea of you." He then went ahead to sip his drink as if he had not said something very hurtful or it could be possible that he had no idea of the impact that his words had made to her. Writers who can arrange words beautifully on paper, can become rather blunt with choice of words when using them verbally. Maybe he did not mean to be harsh and was stating the truth in a flattering way, but it felt like a sharp needle to her heart even if his blunt response was not supposed to be, especially when her break up was still fresh.

Is that what I am? A mere idea in people's head. While such thoughts clouded her mind he added, "You are a beautiful idea, a desire one can want but not pursue." His follow up words made her feel flattered and speechless, so she just stood there not knowing what to say. He continued, "In that regard, I wanted to ask that- I - I wanted to write about you in my next book. I would like to dedicate a ballad about you and your beauty if you would let me." He looked at the ground and then at her, nervously.

This caught her completely off guard and in return no word came out of her mouth. He filled in the silence with his own words, "You don't have to answer me right away, think about it. I hope you give me a positive answer but if it is not then that is also fine. But please think about it. I would only have good words for you." She simply nodded and left smiling to herself feeling flattered.

***

A month had passed since her breakup, a month since Kavya had asked to write about her, a month since her mother had been badgering her about finding a suitable man for her to marry. She couldn't even get a chance to grieve for the relationship that she thought was going to be first and last love. Every day in past one month, her mother had been bringing up a photo of some rich man who is willing to marry her and is also willing to clear the debt of family. Rajmati did not intend on marrying any time soon but even if she was, she did not want that person to feel pressured about helping her family just because they were marrying her.

She would also hear comments being passed like, *"She is so beautiful. I would love to have her as my wife. I don't mind helping her family."*

Or comments like, *"Our Rajmati is so beautiful, men would line up to marry her. Having a wife as beautiful as her would raise their status."*

It was as if men wanted or should want to marry her because they could have an arm candy to show off rather than a wife. It was almost her value lay in her physical appearance rather than herself and her values. She was starting to get annoyed by all these talks of marriage. She no longer knew what to think or feel. That is why that morning, before her mother could approach her with yet another proposal of some rich, old man, she got out of the house to see her friends.

Charu had invited her and Tara over to enjoy some *thwo:*, a milky-looking rice wine that her family was extracting that day. Charu's mother occasionally made *thwo:*, and whenever she did, she would invite her sisters and Charu's friends over for drinks, often preparing a bottle for them to take home as well. Just as Rajmati's father's *ailah:* was renowned, Charu's mother's *thwo:* was cherished by everyone.

When Rajmati reached her friend's place, she noticed from the shoes outside that Tara was already there, so she took off her shoes and rushed directly to Charu's room expecting them to be there. As she walked inside the room, she saw them whispering in a worried tone and as soon as she entered, both of them went quiet at once which made Rajmati curious, so she asked, "What's wrong?"

"It's nothing," both said at the same time. Not believing a single word, she asked again, "No, it is not nothing. You two were clearly talking about something. What is it?"

When they both didn't say anything, she added, "It is about him, isn't it?" referring to Nhugha.

"Don't worry about him," Tara spoke hastily and poured thwo: in a small bowl and pushed it towards Rajmati.

"Yeah, let him be where he is, you know. He is not worth it. If it was so easy for him to leave you and start meeting prospective girl to marry then-" Charu upon realising what she had just said, abruptly brought her hand to her mouth while Tara shook her head in disappointment.

Rajmati couldn't believe what she had just heard so asked again, "What? He is already meeting other girls?"

"He actually has already chosen someone to marry, I think," Charu added reluctantly. The statement broke her all over again and a drop of tear fell but she wiped away quickly and gulped down the entire *thwo:* placed in front of her.

"I am sorry Mati," Charu said making circles in her back when Rajmati did not respond back at all.

"It's- it's alright," she spluttered and moved towards the balcony. Two of the friends nodded in agreement not to follow her, thinking that she might want to be by herself for some time.

While sitting on the *sukul*, flat straw mat, placed in the balcony she looked upon the streets where they grew up.

Young Nhugha always had flower on his ear. He would always look for a reason to talk to her and would always come up with something funny to make her laugh. After confessing his love for her, he started bringing flowers to make her smile. It used to be huge bouquet of flowers at first, then it became smaller bouquet, slowly, it was a lone rose or a single flower that she would adorn on her hair. Then slowly, things started getting complicated between them. There were too many silences and not as many conversations so eventually, he brought sad news to make her cry.

The ringing phone brought her out of the reverie. Her mom spoke before she could, "Eh *machaa*, Nini was mentioning that there is someone who is interested in seeing you for potential marriage. I have seen his photo. He is very handsome and much better than that Tuyucha. Such a good proposal would not come again and again. What do you think? I know you are going to say that you are not ready and want to take some time. But time is going away. I think he is a good match. He is also your father's friend's son and is only a year older than you. Shall I fix a time for families to meet?"

"Sure, go ahead," were the only three words spoken in response to her mother's lengthy ramble which went quiet, quite immediately.

Chapter 10

Rajmati walked into the conversation her mother was having with Nini over the phone.

"I will fix the date for families to meet soon," Rajmati heard the voice of matchmaker from the phone that her mother had put on loudspeaker, probably to make it easier for her to do her kitchen chores while talking on phone.

"Ok, let me know soon, alright. I need to go now," her mother responded back after seeing her and hastily cut the call then, putting the stove on low heat, her mother walked towards her.

Holding her by the arms, her mother said, "I am so happy you agreed with this proposal. It really is a good match no matter what others would have to say. He is a good guy."

"How do you know?" she asked and added, "What do you mean by 'no matter what others would have to say?'" while air quoting her mother's statement.

"I am just worried that others might say we got you married to a rich guy to help ourselves," her mother responded walking away from her and towards the stove to check on the dish.

"And why would they think that? And is it far from the truth?" Rajmati asked sarcastically.

"Machaa," her mother started using endearing term that meant kid, the term she used to call her since Rajmati was little. This time the same endearing word was used more as to make her understand that all of this was particularly important and serious, "He really is a good guy, and I really think you should give him a chance."

"You mean he is not like all the other men who wanted a trophy wife or wanted to rub off how rich they were."

"What are you talking about? Nobody was like that. Most importantly, he is a son of your father's friend. He is a lovely boy. Your father and his father want to do business together. You know family situation. This marriage could be good for the family as much as it is good for you. I know it sounds like too good to be true but at least give him a chance. Don't jeopardize this, please."

"Okay," she said solemnly to which she could see a guilt in her mother's eyes, but no words of consolation came from her mother to ease her mind.

***

Her mother's words ringed in her ears as she saw the stranger walking into the bar. He looked a little lost at first then his eyes landed on her and never left. He had a dusky skin and sharp jawline- he was what women called "tall, dark and handsome." When he smiled looking at her, she couldn't help but smile.

When he came a little closer, she noticed that his amber eyes held a hint of familiarity, but she couldn't tell exactly where she had seen the same pair of eyes before.

"Hi Raani," his first two words that greeted her were enough to remind her who he really was. He smiled looking at her with his arms now resting on the bar top, the only structure separating them both from each other. She remembered the young man she had called friend once— a lifetime ago. His face now held the maturity that lacked in his younger years, and it looked good on him. The eyes and the way he called her "Raani," however, hadn't changed at all. It was his way of teasing her, at least that's what she thought.

"If we were to break down your name into two- Raj and Mati, then that would mean you have a mati to raj, as in destiny to rule. I am just saying this but if what I said is true and if you do have destiny to rule, then you could be Raani, Queen, you know," younger he used to tell her.

They were kid when they made up these meaning out of their names, but he always stuck with calling her Raani. She never stopped him- it made her feel that she really was a Queen even for a briefest of moment.

Both of them grew up in same *tole* until the day he and his family moved out. She was almost thirteen at that time. Later she came to find out from her parents talking to each other that his family had to move to new place because of his father's

68

work. She was sad that he never even came to even say goodbye. Despite studying in different school and having their own group of friends, they always met and caught up around their places after school. They would always visit *Jatras* and festivals in their surroundings together. She still waited for him during festivals, but he never came. At first, she was sad then she was mad at him. When social media was new and everyone were looking for their old friends, she vowed she would not never look for him if he would not look for her. Her pride won at that time. Slowly with times, new friends came along, and new life began where she did not miss him much or so she thought.

When she didn't speak and just looked at him with mix of confusion and surprise colouring her face, he spoke again, "I am not sure if you are trying to recall who I am, or you don't remember me at all, or the worst you are confusing me with someone else."

That must have gotten her out of whatever haze she had been in since seeing him- shaking her head no and putting her loose strand behind, she said, "I am sorry, I do recognise you, but I was not expecting to see you here- not after all these years."

Upon seeing him, she realised that he was never replaced by any of her other friendships— she had just not chosen to relish those memories. His return felt like he was back to take his old place in her life. With all these years behind them, she was not sure if she was still mad at him or happy to meet an old friend.

"I am sorry for that. I am sorry for not being in touch with you," he said. His words felt sincere, and as if all she wanted was to hear that from him, she was now happy to see him and for some reason no longer mad.

"Don't be. I didn't either," she reassured with a smile.

"They say good friendships can get right back where it left off, right?" he said smiling back at her, his eyes full of hope and relief. She wanted to ask him so many things, but she didn't know where to begin.

"Yes, of course, let's start it off with a drink," she proposed, "What would you like to drink?"

He laughed in an amusement and said, "Whatever you would like me to try." She could not help but notice how husky his voice had gotten. Then she remembered how he used to sing while playing guitar at times. She had always enjoyed listening to that.

"So do you still sing?" she asked while preparing his drink.

"You do remember me," he mused, "but that person has changed a little bit. I don't sing anymore." There was a hint of sadness when he said that. She looked up at him in disbelief stopping in the middle of unscrewing a bottle of spirit. She wanted to ask why? And that "why" would be for so many things? Why did you stop singing? Why did you not contact me all this time? Why did you come back suddenly? Why *are* you here?

Before she could speak, he asked, "Would you not want to marry me?" which brought her train of thoughts to a halt, making her lose the grip on the bottle she was holding but thankfully she didn't drop it like couple of glasses she had before he had arrived. She looked away and focused on pouring the alcohol instead of conjuring up words to answer him. She could not process his question properly, then he added, "if I don't sing anymore." He paused and straightened himself up and asked again, "I mean would you still marry me if I don't sing anymore?"

Thinking he might just have been joking; she laughed out loud making onlookers turn their gaze towards them. Ignoring them she joked, "That could have been a dealbreaker."

"I should start singing then," he added further. She no longer knew if he was serious or joking.

She sighed and said, "Well, it doesn't matter anymore."

"Why not?" he asked curiously.

"I am betrothed to another," she said pushing a *salichaa*, a small concave clay cup brimmed with spirit towards him.

He looked at her, a little taken aback from her words and then it looked like something clicked in his mind when he said, "So, you asked to meet your future husband but never asked to see his picture, is it?"

Then suddenly, she understood why he was there. He was here because she had asked him to.

"Do not jeopardise this," her mother's voice rang on her head once again.

Her mother would use the same words every time, Rajmati brought reluctance over this marriage or put up conditions on the marriage proposal. She even refused to see his photo because she was worried that it would make it real. In fact, she did not see any suitors photo, she would

71

just reject them. But in the heat of the moment, she had agreed to meet this suitor. She was not particularly enthusiastic about her bartending job compared to her interest in interior designing, but managing the bar of her parents was something she had to do and was not ashamed of it. If she was going to marry this person, he needed to be someone who valued people and didn't judge them based on their profession or circumstances, so she had the condition for the suitor to see her at her work and be ok with it.

"I won't" she had told her mother, "But he needs to come meet me at the bar if he is to marry me, that is my only condition."

"He is a busy man, why don't you two meet somewhere else perhaps?"

"Nope, if he wants to meet me before marriage, then it would be at the bar. I am a busy woman too."

Her mother had tried really hard to not send her future son-in-law to the bar that is why Rajmati thought that her mother might not have told him about it. It had also been a while since her mother passive aggressively told her that, "You are messing your own life."

Her mother might have mentioned his name in one of their similar backs and forth regarding her suitor to visit her workplace, but she never paid attention because she was certain that the person of his status would not step into her bar or let alone be ok with her working at one.

Her mother's taunts had stopped recently and so was her insistence about changing the meeting location. But now looking at Roman, in front of her, she understood why. She had told her, and he had agreed to visit.

She never in her wildest dreams assumed that it could be her childhood friend; even when he walked in, her mind did not for a slightest moment thought that he could indeed be her suitor. She was just too focused on seeing the friend she hadn't seen for a long time.

"Well, I thought I should just see him in person, rather than in picture, however, I really would have appreciated a bit of heads up," she responded to Roman.

He smiled and said, "I wanted to surprise you. I am now here upon your wish." He then looked at the drink she had pushed towards him earlier.

"Nice choice of cup," he said looking at *salichaa* full of *ailah*.

"We serve our best alcohol in *salichaa*, just the way it should be consumed," she replied and gesturing toward his drink and to the bar she added, "So, do you still want to marry me?"

He was astonished by the suddenness of the question, but he recovered.

"I thought you would never ask," he joked and then added, "Is it some sort of test or something?"

"Well, I felt like you were hesitant when I first asked to be met at my place of work."

"For that I apologise, I was not aware of that. I was told about it only recently and I made sure to come visit immediately. I am sorry again for making you think I didn't want to come or making you doubt about my intention," he elaborated. Rajmati looked at him curiously for his apology and explanation. She then responded back with, "You don't have to apologise. We are here now, and I was just trying to make sure that you are sure of what you are getting into."

"Unlike you, I knew who I was meeting tonight, and I am the one who brought the proposal to marry you, if you didn't know," he replied taking his drink and swirling the salichaa around his hand that held a band of ring in his index finger.

Prying her eyes away from his hand, she asked raising one of her eyebrows, "Even if I work at the bar? Wouldn't it be embarrassing for your image?"

He looked around the crowded bar and turned towards her, "You are running a business like every other business here, why would that be a problem? Even if you were working as a bartender, who am I to hold any judgement around it? It's a job like every other job. I am more proud than embarrassed."

"So, you wouldn't have a problem if I do this even after marriage."

"So, is that a, yes?" he asked teasingly leaving Rajmati speechless, once again that night.

He continued, "It is your choice, Raani. If that is what you want to do, you should. I cannot stop you from doing or not doing anything. May I suggest just one thing though?"

She nodded for him to go ahead.

"My only suggestion is, whether you marry me or not, would you be willing to hire more staff around here so that you can take the rest you need? And I am more than willing to be an investor here." Rajmati started to oppose and before she could say anything, he brought his hand up to speak, "before you hurt your ego because of what I said. I am not doing it out of it or because I am trying to get married to you. I see potential in this business, and I really think we can make it bigger."

"We?"

"Would you not like to be "we"?" he then finally sipped his ailah letting it burn his neck as it passed through his system. He closed his eyes relishing the taste.

She on the other hand looked like the one who was burned by that alcohol and did not know what to say. Before he showed up here, she was certain that whoever her suitor was never going to step into Itumbar but now he was here and ticking all the boxes, she did not what she wanted anymore.

He had never shown slightest hint of his interest towards her in the past, so she was not sure why after all these years of no communication, he was suddenly here to marry her. Knowing that it was someone she knew, did made it bit easier for her to say yes but also hard at the same time, because she didn't know what she was signing up for and wondered if he knew what he was signing up for.

There were so many things that she wanted to ask him, to tell him but she was not ready. She wanted to tell him that she recently broke up with someone, and she was just getting married so that her mother would leave her alone with talks of marriage and also dark part of her heart wanted to show Nhugha that someone did want to marry her despite her line of work. She did not know if Roman deserved such selfish kind of relationship from her but at the same time, she did not know why on earth he suddenly decided to marry her. Her mothers word rang again in her ear, *"Don't jeopardise this."*

So, when he asked her if she was happy with the marriage she just nodded yes.

Chapter 11

Nhugha was visiting the flower shop the same time she was opening the bar. It was bound to happen one day or the other with his shop and her bar opposite to each other. They had successfully avoided each other until last week. She noticed that he looked like he hadn't slept for days. He tried to smile at her and waved slightly. She couldn't bring herself to give any reaction at all so before he could come forward to talk to her, she just walked in.

She got so busy working at the bar, she had forgotten about the earlier interaction but when she was coming outside with bags of trash to put it in the collection bin for the next day, she noticed that someone was standing outside in the dark. She was not sure who it was and did not want to know either. Staying at the same place, she tried looking for keys to put between her fingers to defend herself if needed. As the figure moved closer, it called out for her and to her relief it was the voice of her fiancée.

"Hi," Roman said, and she responded with a sigh of relief and a smile, "Hi, what are you doing here at this time?"

"Well, I knew you were working till late so I thought I would accompany you or help you with anything if needed. I hope I did not scare you," he said trying to make sure she was alright.

She shrugged and said, "No, well, maybe a little but that is because I did not expect anyone out there at this time."

He then took some trash bags from her hand and both of them walked towards the collection bin nearby, "I know, you can handle yourself, but to be honest I just wanted to see you," he replied which made her blush a little.

Not knowing how to respond to that, she instead joked, "This late?"

"I was working till late as well tonight so I could arrive only now, otherwise I would have arrived even earlier," he said and dropped the trash bags into the bin. Not wanting to show her reaction to his words, she walked towards the nearby tap to wash her hands. Roman followed her and washed his hand after she was done. Then wiping his hand with his handkerchief, he turned towards her and said, "I also wanted to check with you if you were truly ok with bringing the wedding forward. I am sorry to rush this. My parents are being insistent on this for some reason. Probably because, I might have to leave for couple of months to go to Sydney for business trip, but nothing is set yet. I think they just want to make sure I don't walk away from my word. Not that I would. I would never."

She chuckled at his continuous trail of explanation but before she could respond anything, someone called her name, name by which nobody had called her since her breakup.

"Rati!"

Both Roman and Rajmati looked at the direction of the voice, a small alley in their right.

"Nhugha?" she asked in surprise.

"I just wanted to talk to you. I tried earlier but you went in, so I waited here," Nhugha said.

"In this dark alley?" Roman questioned raising one of his eyebrows.

"Who is he?" Nhugha asked Rajmati without acknowledging Roman.

"He is my fiancée," she replied leaving both men in surprise. Among them, however, only one man was pleasantly surprised.

"Oh," Nhugha responded, still ignoring Roman and turning to Rajmati, he said, "I just wanted to tell you that I am really sorry for how things had to end between us. I just want to bring closure. I hope you forgive me and understand why we had to break up."

She couldn't comprehend why he was saying that now. Maybe he just wanted to take it off his chest and if the dark circle under his eyes were to be believed, he might have been troubled with it. But doing this now in front of Roman did not make sense either and this irritated her further.

"Is that all?" she asked bluntly.

"Don't you have anything to say to me?" he asked with shock induced from her nonchalance.

"We are both moving on with our lives. There is nothing left to talk about," she responded looking at him and turning her gaze towards Roman, she spoke gently, "Shall we Roman?" and walked away from the scene but before they could even take a step, Nhugha spoke, "Is that why you are marrying in such a rush- to forget me?"

Roman clenched his jaw and his hands were now ball of fist and seemed to be having tough time controlling his anger, so before he could say or do anything, Rajmati spoke without turning back to look at Nhugha, "Is that why you are?"

"Don't you know why?" he said like a boy who was going to start a tantrum if he did not get what he wanted.

"I don't need to answer any of your questions. You did what you did. Let me go."

She held Roman's hand and walked ahead, the action letting him loosen the fist and hold onto her tightly yet gentle.

Later she turned towards Roman and said, "I am sorry you had to witness that. He is-"

"Your ex-boyfriend?" he completed her sentence.

"Yes, if you couldn't tell," she responded sarcastically but aware he might have lots of questions regarding this.

"You don't need to apologise. I just want to know if you are alright. Are you okay and is everything alright?" he asked.

"Yes, it is. I have been fine for a while now. I have been wanting to tell you before actually, but I did not know how to bring it up. We broke up recently but to be honest we were falling apart quite a long time ago."

"Do you still want to be with him? By the looks of recent interaction, it seems like you don't. I am just asking for the sake of it," he said.

"I don't. I am sorry I didn't tell you before."

"Please don't say sorry, Raani. Everyone has a past and as long as I am your present. I would rather not have such trivial things affect us."

She looked at him in awe, still wondering why he wanted to marry her.

"So, are you okay with moving the date ahead?" he asked with a smile.

"Yes," she smiled and nodded. The answer came quite naturally this time than it was when he had asked before.

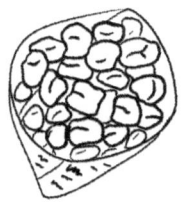

Chapter 12

"You have such a beautiful voice, the girl you would marry would be so lucky," she had said once.

"And why is that?" he had asked.

"Because you would serenade her with your music and songs?" she replied directing her hands toward the guitar in his arms.

"I don't think anybody would want to marry me," he sighed putting his guitar away.

"If nobody marries you then I will if you promise to sing to me every day," she joked making both of them laugh.

***

Laakhaa had arrived her home almost immediately after Rajmati had agreed to marry Roman. She watched them bring all the beautifully decorated trays full of different items from daily essentials for the new bride to gold jewelleries. She was lost in thought and did not know how to feel about what was happening and all the rush that was coming with it.

The rush of marriage preparations came and went like heavy whoosh of a wind. One after another, events happened and went by like a montage in a movie. If she did not have a photograph as evidence, she would not know if some of the events even happened. Some moments were very distinct while some were blurry. After pre wedding, wedding and post wedding events, bride and groom were close to losing their social battery.

Next thing they knew, they were in an enclosed room just the two of them. They had been married for about five days now but as per customs, there were several other post wedding traditions before they could be in the same room together.

They both sat on the bed awkwardly in silence. They have been in noise and chaos of wedding for so long, the silence made them feel rather vulnerable and perhaps too aware of their own breathing. They looked at each other and as their eyes met, they couldn't help but smile.

He slowly moved his hand towards hers and held her hand in his. She looked up at him unsure and a little nervous but the moment her eyes met his, she knew that his eyes held lots of love and respect for her. She didn't know how she saw that, but she could feel it in her heart and her bones.

He looked down and slightly strengthening the hold on hers he spoke, "I know we have lost so many years between us and there is so much we do not know about each other, so I don't want for us to rush this. I want to us know each other all over again as a husband and a wife." Husband and wife, the words felt too real and too strange at the same time in her ears, so she attempted to joke, "Isn't it too late for that?"

"Is it? I would still like to know each other. I am sorry we had to rush this wedding and ceremonies, but I do not want to rush our entire marriage. I want to get to know you and for you to know me if that is alright with you."

She smiled upon his words and suddenly all the awkwardness washed away, when she spoke, "I would love that."

"Thank you," with that he slightly pulled her towards him and kissed her forehead.

"You look tired, you should get some sleep," Roman said next.

"You too," she responded yawning. She got up from the bed, her bangles and clothes making beautiful sound out of it with all the little bells and jingles in them. He smiled at the sound and got up to freshen up as well. When he was out of the bathroom in his nightwear looking fresh, she was in front of a mirror in her robe, struggling with her hair.

He moved towards her and started taking out pins from her hair. With her hand paused midair, she looked up at him in surprise. He looked at her through mirror and asked, "Is it alright if I help you with this?" She nodded with a smile.

He started piling all the pins on top of the dressing table that held her bangles strewn haphazardly on top. As he worked on her hair, she started removing her makeup. Suddenly he stopped looking at the redness on her wrist and asked, "What's wrong with your wrist and hands? Why is it all red?"

"Oh, it's the bangles. It was bit tight when I was trying to remove so the skin got bit irritated, that's all," she replied nonchalantly but he still seemed to be worried.

After her hair was free and makeup removed, she spoke, "So, this is the real me, are you scared of it?"

"If anything you look even more beautiful," he said tucking her curly strand behind her ears. He put his hand on her hair a little too long.

She cleared her throat and spoke, "I will go freshen up." He nodded.

"You have not slept yet?" she asked Roman who seemed to be arranging her bangles and other items in place when she came out of the bathroom in her baby blue silk pyjamas while drying her hair with the towel. The other option was red night gown which she did not feel appropriate despite it being their "wedding night."

"No, I was looking for a moisturiser actually so thought of arranging these while I was looking for it," he said searching around.

"I didn't know you had a night care routine," she said smiling and took out the moisturiser from one of the many bags on the floor and gave it to him.

"Oh no, it's not for me, it is for you," he said turning around to face her and was about to say something, but he paused, stunned momentarily looking at his wife while she looked at him unaware of what was happening in his mind. He took the tub from her and cleared his throat.

"For your hands. I thought it would soothe your skin where the bangles hurt you," he said opening the lid and giving it back to her.

"Oh, thank you," she replied taking back the now open tub of moisturising cream from his hand and applied it on her skin.

"You should dry your hair. You will get a headache if you sleep with a wet hair," he said, and she nodded.

That night, they both slept next to each other sticking to their side of the bed. Though their body were next to each other, their mind and soul far apart from each other.

***

The next morning, they found themselves sitting next to one other having warm tea and *Gwarmari*, for the breakfast. With his family living away from the valley, it was only going to be Roman and Rajmati living in the penthouse. He had lots of work in the city, so he decided to get himself an apartment in the heart of city at the highest skyscraper overlooking the valley.

He had chosen to live in the middle of the city because of his work while the rest of the family wanted to stay a little away from the hustle and bustle.

"Gwarmari is so good. Perfect for this morning," Rajmati exclaimed appreciating the food.

Roman responded back with a smile saying, "I am glad you loved it." Roman had gone out in the morning and bought fresh Gwarmari from the local shop around the corner. As she relished on the fried dough, he felt satisfied.

After a moment of silence, Roman spoke again, "If any of this interior is not to your liking, please feel free to change them as you see fit."

"Are you not worried that I might change your living space no sooner than I have arrived here," she joked.

"Not at all. I trust you with your choices. I am not married to this space, but I am married to you so whatever my Raani chooses, I am sure, I will love it. It was just a house for me before you walked in here but now it already feels like home."

She blushed not understanding how this person trusts her with these things and say all these lovely words. "You look even more beautiful when you smile," he added without realising while being lost in her beauty.

She coughed and as an attempt to change the topic, she asked, "So tell me, what were you up to when you were in Sydney?"

The question might have got him off guard, so she added, "You mentioned we have lost years' worth of time, and we should get to know each other, so this is my attempt at it."

He chuckled and said, "Well, I went there to study and at one point I was planning to stay there but then I decided to come back."

"And why is that?"

"I got a better opportunity here."

She raised her eyebrows his in disbelief and said, "That is rare."

"That is true. My cousin brother had this idea he wanted to pursue, and I wanted to invest on it. At the same time, I saw the potential of running real estate business in a different way than it has been going on here so I thought I could try my luck here first and with *Digudya's* blessing, it flourished. I have been doing back and forth between here and Sydney for last couple of years because of new business I have started there, but this is the longest I had stayed back. I would love to take you there one day."

She nodded and asked, "You are travelling there soon, aren't you?"

"It was going to be in a couple of weeks, but I have postponed it. The work here is getting bit hectic, so I need to sort it out first."

"Oh, ok. I hope everything is alright, not anything drastic, I hope," she sympathized.

"Nothing that cannot be resolved," he said with reassuring smile then leaning his both arms against the table he asked, "So, you tell me, what got you into bartending when you have a degree in interior designing?"

"Honestly, I had to take care of the bar because there was no other choice. I had always wanted to work on interiors, assimilating both traditional and modern looks. I did that with the bar and small projects here and there but ultimately; I had to choose between the bar or continuing with my passion for designs. The bar had to be managed by someone, so——."

"Why didn't your dad manage it?" he asked.

"He wanted to, but he kept on getting sick time and again. He still made *ailah* but that itself took too much of his energy, so I stepped in," she explained.

"You have done an excellent job with it, I mean both interior and the bar itself. Why don't you hire a managing staff as well to look after it and focus on interior designing completely? I would love your expertise on some of the houses I am working on."

She just nodded with a smile.

Suddenly, the phone started ringing but Roman ignored it. When it continued ringing, he apologised to Rajmati and took the call. Roman was now busy on his phone pacing around the room with sparing words of "Now?" "It's alright" "Ugh...I will see what I can do?"

"What happened?" Rajmati asked him when he put down the phone.

"I need to go to office to sort out an issue. I am so sorry," he said walking towards Rajmati.

"It is alright. You should go," she responded nodding her head.

"I will try to come back as soon as possible," he said rushing to the bedroom to get ready.

After few moments, he came back changed from his sweatpants to white shirt and black suit pant. This time it was Rajmati who was momentarily stunned looking at her husband. Rajmati stood up and went to give him his keys which he seemed to be looking for her. He thanked her and moved towards the door, "I have one business to attend but I will be home soon. I am sorry I did not mean to go to work today. I was on leave but something urgent came up. Call me if you need anything."

She nodded in understanding. Just as he was by the door, he came back in, making her turn toward him. He leaned in and gave her a gentle kiss on the cheek, leaving her blushing in her new home as she traced her fingers where his lips had been a moment ago. She felt a swirl of emotions—confusion and uncertainty about all the recent changes creeping into her mind. She never got to ask him why he wanted to marry her and probably it was too late for that question. Now, as the haze was settling down, she was not sure if it was the right decision.

Ever since he had left tole and especially after moving abroad, they had barely kept in touch. Now, to suddenly reappear in her life and ask for her hand in marriage—it was baffling. She agreed to marry him under the pressure from her family, and she did not want him to get the impression that she took advantage of him so she decided to be the dutiful wife even if she may never be able to love him. She was not even sure if he loved her either. It was just a marriage of convenience for them both. Yet, she still couldn't fathom what he stood to gain from marrying her.

Chapter 13

A one-of-a-kind social event was happening in Kathmandu valley with the presence of socialites and people with heavy influence. The venue had the essence of history that Ranas left behind and hint of modernism that modern world had brought in. Though it looked like a building which was built by historical aristocrats, it was, in reality, a fairly new building made very recently by one of the richest of the valley.

It was supposed to be an intimate event; however, it looked more like a networking event with everyone introducing themselves and their business, exchanging business cards and their potential partnership. There were also few who did not need a show of rectangular piece of paper to indicate who they were. For them, their presence in this event was enough. They need not even move around the room. For them the room was static and around them, people would swarm effortlessly.

When Roman and Rajmati entered the venue, all eyes turned towards them. While Roman was wearing black and

91

white tuxedo with pocket square made of dhaka fabric, Rajmati was adorned in black and red saree with blouse made from dhaka fabric. When they entered, many eyes were on them. Most of them were curious to see who the elusive bachelor Roman got married to, while some wanted to confirm if the rumours were true— that he really was married to the beauty of the town that many had sought, and many families denied. Nevertheless, people could not deny the fact that they looked quite a pair— stunning and gorgeous by themselves but equally powerful together.

As they move through the party, they met the host and gradually met whom they needed to meet.

"Wow, you have a truly beautiful wife, Roman," exclaimed a middle-aged man when Roman walked towards him. He laughed a little and greeted him.

"Namaste, Balram dai, what can I say, I have been blessed with not only beautiful but a very smart lady to call my wife."

"That's good, that's good but bragging too much is not a nice thing," the elderly man grumbled.

"I am not bragging, I am just agreeing with you, ha-ha," Roman replied. They went on with their conversation for a while longer and moved ahead.

The pleasantries continued and throughout these exchanges, Rajmati could not help but notice that most people were surprised to see Roman married and went ahead to exaggerate how beautiful his wife was. While some really appreciated them as couple, many gave rather judgemental look towards her.

She was coming outside of the restroom when she overheard some men and women talking, "That Roman, got a really beautiful wife, huh?" the voice of the man, sounded rather slurred and croaky.

"And he paid quite the money to have a trophy wife. I mean look at her, having such a beauty does show some standard, doesn't it?" she heard another voice of a man who sounded rather young than the previous one.

"It probably helps with building connection too," this time it was a voice of a woman with a very sultry tone.

"Oh no no, I heard, his family was kicked out of the tole they were living in and no one wanted to give their daughter to him, so she was his last resort," another woman with a sharp voice spoke.

"Oh my god, I think you need to stop watching these tele series now. Who thinks of such things in real life?" said the previous young man.

"Probably he just needed to show everyone here that prettiest of women are lining up to marry him. To brag you know. Men and their ego, who knows and having a trophy wife does not hurt," the sultry voice chimed again.

"I don't see any sort of spark between them. Do you? I heard it was marriage of money and convenience," the croaky man spoke.

"I think you need to stop drinking. You are making up weird stories now."

Rajmati felt like emptying the content of her stomach upon hearing that. She moved away from the conversation, not wanting to hear anymore and not really understanding what to think or how to react.

***

"Is everything alright?" Roman asked her again and she just nodded like previous three times upon his same question. The recent conversations that she had overheard was revolving around her head. She was neither smiling nor she was in awe as much as she was when she arrived.

Sensing the change in her mood, perhaps, he asked, "Shall we go home?"

She nodded and went towards the exit of the venue without bidding goodbye to anyone.

By the time they reach home, Rajmati those conversation and random thoughts were taunting her, so much so that it triggered the question she had in her mind for a long time.

Why did he want to marry me?

"Raani, is everything alright? You seem lost." Roman asked with concern when she had been very silent in the car and all the way to home.

"Huh," she asked lost in thoughts.

"Are you okay?" he asked, his concern for her rising by the second.

94

She rushed the words of assurance, "Yes, yes, of course, I am ok." Walking inside the penthouse, Roman was not certain, if she was fine as she claimed.

"You can talk to me if anything is bothering you," he said. She gave half a smile and moved towards their room. He followed her, then suddenly she turned and crashed into his hard chest, his hands rushed to hold her from falling and his eyes searching if she was truly alright.

She apologised, "Sorry, I didn't realise you were right behind me."

"I always will be, if it helps," he said solemnly.

She half expected him to be teasing her, but his face reflected that he meant what he just said. It almost felt like a promise that he would be there for her, and she would never have to feel alone. She straightened herself and moved away from him.

"Can I ask you something?" she spoke now sitting down on a stool in front of her dressing table.

"Sure," he said taking out the cuff links from his shirt and walking towards the closet.

She took out her heavy earrings and contemplating a little, she finally asked, "Why did you marry me?"

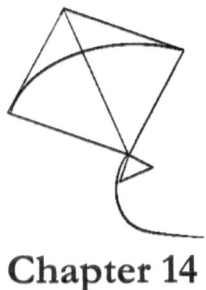

Chapter 14

The days were warmer and longer, people were preparing for the upcoming plantation season. There is a belief in Kathmandu valley that no kites should be flown in the sky during or before plantation season. It should only be flown during Dashain when farming season would be over because flying the kites was like sending a message to the God of Rain, Indra that we had enough of rain for the year. So, farmers would get concerned and incredibly angry if they saw people flying kites ahead of the season; they would worry that they would not get enough rain.

Roman and his friend Ratna, both the age of nine at that time, were in the middle of the field flying kites. It was Saturday so they had the entire day to themselves.

Ratna lived in different neighbourhood than Roman but on most Saturdays, they would visit each other to play around and this time to fly kite. They flew kite for an hour trying to put each of their kite further away in the sky. After a bunch of banters and talking about kite facts, they relaxed and brought their kites to the ground.

96

Roman took out a packet of instant fried noodle from his bag and after putting in the spices that came with it, he extended it to Ratna. Ratna took handful of noodles from the packet and put it in his mouth and Roman did the same—the crunching sound of noodles filling the air. After finishing the packet of noodle and a bottle of water, Roman said, "Let's fly the kite, again."

"I need to go home early today, so I need to leave now," Ratna spoke gathering his items.

"Already?" Roman said with disappointment.

"Yeah, my house is bit far from here, and my mom said not to be late, so I need to run," he said packing his kite, after a moment, he looked at Roman who looked rather sad to end this day early so Ratna said, "But how about I help you fly your kite and then I will leave."

Roman nodded excitedly. Ratna pulled the kite away from Roman and pushed it upward to help it catch the wind and there it went up in the sky again.

"I will see you at school," Ratna said and waved goodbye taking his kite with him. Roman just waved and continued working the thread of the spool, staring at his lone kite in the bright blue clear sky. After a while he got bored and started retracting the thread to bring it back to the ground.

The kite was in the mid-air when he heard someone screaming, "Oi, Kid, what the hell do you think you are doing? Flying a kite before Dashain. Don't you know you shouldn't fly kites this early on." He turned to see that there was a huge old man looking at his direction angrily. He was bit far from him, so Roman still had time to grab his things and make a run. Soon, the old man grabbed a stick from the ground and strode quickly towards Roman. He hurriedly retracted his kite and ran hastily with mud splattering all over his trousers.

97

Suddenly a small hand grabbed his wrist then pulled him towards a narrow pathway that led to a small shelter. He was completely taken aback because it was not the bulky man who caught him but a little girl with messy curls and muddy legs holding him and helping him hide. They heard the voice again making both the kids flinch, "Where did he go? These days kids just don't know anything."

They waited silently in their hiding spot until they heard the sound of stick thrown to the ground and retreating footsteps. They both sighed in relief and the girl said, "I think we should wait a little before we go out again." He only nodded.

"We live in the same neighbourhood," she said, and he again nodded.

"I am Rajmati, by the way," she said extending her hand.

He just stared at her in shock leaving her hand hanging in the air. She then used the same hand to wave in front of him and when he still did not respond, she felt awkward and her smile faltered but something in his little kid heart felt bad to see her smile turning into frown, so he quickly said, "I know. I am Roman."

When Rajmati arrived in the tole for the first time, a couple of months ago, every kid wanted to be her friend. He used to be friends with those kids but because of Roman's grumpiness kids eventually stopped playing with him, since then he only played in school with his school friends or stayed at home looking at his former friends from the window of his house. He sometimes would come at chowk, the communal area and watched them play but he did not have any intention of playing with them and neither did the other kids had any intention to play with him. He had thought of talking to her once, but she was always surrounded by friends and laughing around so he did not approach her at all.

Little did he know, she had noticed him and had wondered why he didn't play with everyone.

98

As they sat on the muddy ground under small alcove of the bridge she asked, "Why do you not hang out with our friends in the tole?"

He shrugged and said, "Because I don't like being surrounded by people."

"So would you rather hangout with one friend at a time?" she asked.

He nodded.

"Can I then be that one friend when your other friend is not here?" she asked innocently.

"Sure," he said without smiling, but she smiled widely with one tooth missing at front. That smile brightened her face and for some reason warmed his heart. She then extended her hand and this time he took it with a slight shy smile.

They did not become close friends immediately, but they started saying hi to each other whenever they passed one another ever since that day. The years passed by, they grew up and so did their friendship. As they went to different school in different grades, they had their own group of friends but almost every day after school, they would meet up, roam around the tole and if there were any Jatras happening in the tole, they would always go there together to watch it. They would share their school stories, sing songs, and end up being each other's closest friend until that day when he did not come looking for her after school or to that Jatra, they always went together. He seemed to have vanished like he never existed.

***

She was now looking at his reflection in the mirror. He had now turned around and was looking at her with mixture of confusion and curiosity.

"Because I wanted to marry you," he shrugged with a smile.

"Ok but why did you want to marry me? What do you gain from this?" the words left her mouth before she could stop it and regretted it almost immediately.

Her words turned his smile to frown. He looked at her in shock, not quite understanding why she said what she said. Before she could retract her words, he spoke, "Why would you say that?"

As much as the conversation she overheard seemed absurd, she couldn't help but taint her mind with it. She did not say anything and just stared down at the items in her dressing table. He then slowly approached her and asked, "What is going on in your mind, Raani?"

Raising her gaze from the table but refusing to look at him, she hesitated a little before asking, "Did you just want to showcase me as your wife to show off to your rich fri-"

"Where is this even coming from?," he interrupted her and continued gently, "I just wanted you to take you there for you to enjoy. I wanted to gauze out the eyes of every man looking at you. We don't have to go to these events at all if it makes you uncomfortable. You have no idea how much I hated men staring at you despite knowing you were married to me." He paused for a moment and then asked, "Who was it?"

"I...I don't know. I just overheard," she muttered and got up from her chair and tried to move away from him, but he held on to her wrists gently as if pleading to stay. She turned towards him, both now standing and facing each other, with eyes full of questions. She finally spoke, "I am not vain, but I used to hear people say that the only reason someone would marry me was because of my looks— that they wanted a beautiful wife to show off, probably because they thought that my family did not have much to offer. It was as if I was nothing more than a pretty face, as if I had no personality, soul, or thoughts of my own for that matter."

Then, she looked at the floor and continued, "And when I heard overheard similar conversation about us today, it triggered all those memories and all the questions." Unable to bear the hurt in her voice, he pulled her into a hug and whispered, "You know that's not true, right?"

He then took a step back and looking at her, he explained, "I assure you; I did not marry you just because you are beautiful. Beautiful, you are but that is not the reason to marry someone." His reaction was not something that she was expecting at all. She half-expected him to be angry or walk away from this conversation.

"Then why?" she asked uncertain of where they stand.

"Why are you asking me this question now? Why did you think we got married?" he asked.

"Because our parents wanted us to get married?" she posed the statement like a question.

"It was not my parents' idea. It was mine," the answer he gave left her startled.

She then asked, "But why now? After all this time. Why me?"

Because it was always you.

Then holding onto her arms gently, he said, "I married you because I love you." The confession she never expected from him— the confession somehow more hurtful than what she assumed. She looked at him in surprise while he continued, "I have been in love with you for a very long time. As a child I called it a crush. Growing up I named it infatuation.

I don't know why but it is not just because you are such a beautiful person, not because you saved me from that farmer the first day we talked or because we used to be friends when we were little. I have seen your kindness. I have seen your raw emotions, I have seen you angry, I have seen you happy and, in every version, I have loved you. All this time, I had wanted to be a person who is good enough for you, well to do enough to be someone who deserves you and that is why it took so long for me to get back to you. At one point in my life, I thought you must hate me or worst, you might have forgotten me. I was scared to learn the answer to that one, so I refused to ask. But when I saw you again at the same place, lost in thought, all of those feelings came rushing back in and I couldn't help it. I hated to see how sad you were. It wrenched my heart. I realised then that whatever feeling I had for you, it hadn't gone. I was and am still in love with you."

He was almost 14 years old when his family had to move to another city because of his father's job in *Napi Bibhag-* Department of Survey. It might have been something that his parents knew for some time, but kids are not involved in such decisions so for Roman it had felt like a sudden and abrupt decision. One day he was returning from school, next day he and his family was moving to another city. He wanted to go and tell Rajmati about it, but he never got the chance to. Last time he saw her was from a rolled-up window in a taxi— she was talking with her friends and laughing together reading something on the piece of paper. He etched that memory into his heart.

The thought of her never really left him even when he left the tole to move to another locality, even when he moved to completely another continent to study and start a business. He might have had lovers in different parts of his life, but he still could not bring to get her out of his mind. Assuming his own feelings for her to be just an infatuation, he even tried to forget her.

He refrained himself from getting in touch with her in all these years even when there was rise of social media and people tried to look for their long-lost friends. He was scared to find out that she would no longer remember him. After each passing time, he would think to himself that he had moved on, his memories of her were starting to fade like an old photograph barely surviving the harshness of weather. Little did he know that those memories never faded.

He was just back from Sydney. He was walking towards the dirt pathway that led him to a beautiful garden full of seasonal flowers, park benches and a big gazebo in the middle. There also was a small temple on one side where devotees were passing by. He then remembered there used to be *dhungedhara* nearby because it was the same place where he had seen her last time talking to her friends while he was leaving without a goodbye. Looking around the place he realised that the place had changed a lot— it looked more sophisticated and taken care of than it was before. He wondered where she would be at this time and hoping if he would get a glimpse of her at the same place, he turned around trying to find that *dhungedhara.*

Then suddenly, as if his wish was being granted, he saw her. He recognised her almost at once, but he could not believe his own eyes. After all these years of silence, he was frozen in place looking at the beauty of town, her curls untamed as always, wind blowing against her face, looking more gorgeous than last time, he had seen her. And what a fateful day to see her, Matina Paru: nevertheless. His eyes never left her while his feet stood still unmoving. The wind blew once again, rushing her hair away from her, she didn't attempt to hold it. She raised her head a little revealing her beautiful brown eyes and despite being away from her, he saw the hurt instead of joy in her eyes. He didn't know if he should walk towards her or away from her after disappearing from her life.

That night when he reached home, he couldn't get her out of his mind and regretted not walking towards her; not asking if she was alright and what made her so sad.

"I might not be the same person you left behind," she spoke after a while.

"It does not matter. I love your past, your present and future and every variation of you, Raani."

She gasped upon his confession but unable to look into his eyes, she turned her gaze towards the floor. After all the confession he had made, she could not help but feel sad. She had no knowledge of his feeling for, and she was not sure if she would ever be able to return that feeling.

Then, sudden realisation hit her, what if the matchmaker and her mother insisted him to help the family if she were to marry him because of his feelings for her. She gently pressed on his hand and asked, "Please don't take this the wrong way

104

but did the matchmaker trick you to help my family if you were to marry me?"

"No, she did not trick me, but it was more like I challenged her," he said confusing Rajmati.

"What do you mean?"

He then said, "When matchmaker that my mom hired was tired of me rejecting every girl possible, she had asked me, 'Who are you really looking for, seriously? Or do you not want to marry at all?' My mother had looked at me worryingly and to avoid the question, I told them that I wanted to marry you, only you. I challenged her saying that she would not be able to make it happen. I honestly believed that she would never be able to arrange it, because there would be throngs of people lining up for you, my chances were minimal, but I was still hopeful."

***

"Rajmati," he had said leaving both his mother and matchmaker stunned. He smirked knowing that she would not be able to make it happen. As if his smirk felt like a challenge to her, the matchmaker smiled back confidently and said, "I will get back to you on that one." She left and came back after a week.

"I come bearing good news for you. She has agreed to marry you," the matchmaker spoke rather excitedly congratulating him.

He smiled a little not really believing the words.

"Oh *baucha*, are you listening or not? She has agreed to marry you. Should I prepare for families to meet to fix the date?" the matchmaker spoke again.

At that moment, he wondered if Rajmati even remembered him, so he had asked, "Can I meet her once before we move further with anything?"

"Kids, these days, fine, I will talk to her mother today and ask if you two can meet first."

Ever since that day he had been asking the same question, "So when can I meet her?" while the matchmaker had been dismissing it with phrases like 'she had forgotten to ask' or 'couldn't get hold of her mother.' He would have gone to see her at her home, but he wanted her to agree to meet him first.

"Well," the matchmaker said slowly one time.

"Does she not want to meet me?" he asked to which she hastily waved her hands, "No, no it's not like that. She does actually, but" and rather reluctantly she added, "she said that she would like for you to meet her at the bar where she works."

"Sure," he said getting up, surprising her, completely.

"You will go to see her in the bar?" she asked again.

"Yeah, why not?"

"No, I just thought you would not like to go there."

"Is that why you were not telling me, because you thought I wouldn't go there?"

***

Roman walked towards Rajmati who was now standing by the window and holding her hand, he said, "When the matchmaker asked who I wanted to marry. Your name just blurted out without any effort like I was spitting the fact I had known for long time as if I hadn't hidden that fact from myself all this time."

She held onto his hand and just stared at him not knowing what to say next while her mind was convoluted with the things she had heard throughout the night including the one that Roman was saying.

"Also, she did not mention anything about your family situation. My dad however mentioned that he wanted to partner up with your dad and it all aligned well, us getting married and their venture also coming together. It was rather a coincidence not a condition," he said easily. Continuing to hold her hand, he brought her to the edge of the bed and both of them sat together looking at each other.

This also made her wonder if her was aware that this venture was already happening or if her mother used this as an opportunity to get her married and emotionally manipulate her. He must have noticed the shock in her eyes therefore he couldn't help but ask the question he never wanted to ask, "Why did you agree to marry me? She did not force you to marry me with that condition, did she?"

"I was not aware of your feelings," she whispered, her voice barely audible.

"Why did you really marry me?" he asked again.

Because I had to.

She hesitated first.

She cleared her throat not knowing how to put the next words together, "To be honest, I had given it up to fate. I was not ready to marry at all— to anyone. I was really hurt and in different emotional state when I said yes to meeting the suitor that turned out to be you. I did not even bother to know who the person was. I just could not bear my mother nagging me one more day. I just needed her to shut up about it and it seemed like marrying someone was only way to do it. But if I had to marry someone, I wanted him to be someone who would marry me despite the fact I sold alcohol in a bar. When you came to bar, I was relieved— not because you met my condition but because it was you. I was relieved to know that the person I was going to marry was at least the person I know, and I understand that it was selfish of me to say yes to marriage based on this alone, but I was not aware of your feelings for me. I am sorry."

He looked at her; his face showing equal part concern and equal part hurt.

The silence prevailed in the room; a silence that comes after a huge thunder.

He started pacing around the room, not knowing what to say to what she had just said while she sat on the edge of their bed looking at him eyes full of concern. She then said, "I do care about you, and I am grateful that it was you that I said yes to."

He stopped pacing and he looked at her, a lone tear escaped her eyes, and he rubbed it away immediately. He ran his hand over his hair. He took a long breath and spoke, "I wanted you to marry me willingly. Just having you willingly be part of my life is enough but knowing that it was not entirely your will changes things. You are not an object for me to trade. I need you to understand that this is not a marriage of convenience."

"I did marry you willingly but…"

"But you don't love me," he said with a smile and eyes full of hurt.

She stood speechless not knowing what to say.

"I thought you didn't either. I thought we were just doing what our parents asked us to do. Isn't that what arranged marriage is? I am sorry I am just overwhelmed with all this information."

Her words suddenly changed his demeanour. It was shift from anxiousness to concern as if her words, her being overwhelmed was the last thing he wanted to happen, so he blurted out, "I am sorry for tonight and everything leading to this marriage. Please don't stress over this. We will sort it out. You should get some sleep."

Chapter 15

When she woke up after the night full of confession, he was nowhere to be seen but had left a note saying, "I am sorry, I had to leave early for work today but there might be some guests visiting later."

He had not mentioned anything about who the guests were and why he would invite guest over when he was not even going to be here. When she went downstairs to open the ringing bell, she did not have to wonder for long. He had invited her friends over and made himself scarce for the day.

"What a pleasant surprise," she looked at her two best friends in delight.

"Well, your husband suggested that we visit you and spend some girl time. And it is not like we did not want to visit you; we just thought that you two would want, you know, some couple time so didn't want to disturb you two," Charu teased Rajmati. She invited them inside and showed them around.

"You have a got a really lovely place. You are one lucky girl," Tara exclaimed as she walked inside taking in the surroundings.

Rajmati did not say anything and just nodded smiling.

"What's wrong? Something is wrong. Is he not a good husband?" Tara asked with concern.

"No, no it is nothing like that. Let's just sit down. Do you two want any tea, coffee?" Rajmati asked.

"Tea please and don't bring any snacks, because we brought Jeri Swaari Haluwa from your favourite *Mari: pasa*, breadshop," Charu said walking towards the dining table and placing the plastic bag in the table.

Jeri Swari Haluwa is one of the traditional snacks and breakfast items. Jeri is a sweet delicacy made mostly out of sugar, with a glossy texture, while Swaari is an oily thin flatbread and Haluwa is a dessert made from wheat flour fried in ghee.

Charu and Tara help set up the table and took out all the food items from its bag while Rajmati brought and served tea for three of them.

"So, tell us, what got you so gloomy that you don't seem excited with the breakfast we brought you?" Charu asked while carefully spreading haluwa on Swaari and putting Jeri on top, creating a layered sweet wrap.

"It is nothing really. Thank you for bringing these," Rajmati replied taking the swaari and putting it on her plate.

Tara while taking a sip of her tea, said, "We know something is up. So just spill."

Rajmati took a deep breath and then she proceeded to tell them what had happened last night while her friends listened attentively.

"Now, I don't know what to say to him or face him," Rajmati said at the end.

"He sounds very lovely and respectful. Maybe you will learn to love him?" said Tara sounding not so confident and took another sip of her tea.

"What if I never fall for him!" she exclaimed.

"Sometimes in marriage, respect is enough," Charu added, "Maybe that respect will help last the relationship. Try to rekindle your friendship with him and who knows maybe you will learn to love him."

"I am not sure if I will ever be able to love again," she turned towards her friends, "I no longer want to deal with these messy feelings."

"He is your husband. You have to move on from your previous relationship. He is willing to give you space. Why don't you be a little willing to give him a chance? He does not seem that bad," Tara expressed.

"This is marriage Mati, it is not as simple as other relationships to break up and move on. Also, love can be messy, but it can be a beautiful mess and with marriage thrown into mix its ought to be exciting. There must be a reason you two were brought together," Charu spoke.

"Tuyucha never understood you or valued you. He had been taking you for granted Razz, stop letting him control this next chance at love and relationship you have got," Charu said.

"I do appreciate Roman, and he values me but if I am not able to love him then isn't he missing out on love and all the beautiful things he deserves by being stuck with me?"

"Then at least give him a chance. Give this relationship a chance. Our parents' relationship was arranged too. They learned to love each other. Maybe there is a hope here and he already loves you. Him asking us to join you for the breakfast here so that you get to talk to your friends after the big revelation from last night's conversation, speaks volumes on how he cares about you and your mental health.," Charu said.

Tara spoke slowly after a moment, "Why would you refrain yourself from such beautiful feelings? Wouldn't it be giving more power to that person who never understood your value?"

Tara's words resonated with Rajmati for a long time.

***

She could not help but consider words of her friends from their conversation in the morning. She had no intention of going to bar that day, so she stayed at home stewing over her thoughts and arranging and rearranging items she had ordered online. She reached his study while looking for a stapler and as she was going through the drawers, a folder slipped from her hands dropping several loose papers from it. She rushed to pick them up and while doing so, she noticed that these papers consisted of sketches of someone. As she looked closely, she realised that it was she from her younger years.

113

When she looked at the signature, she learned that it was drawn by Roman and when she calculated the date under that signature, she found out it was long after he had left the tole. Then the realisation hit her that he drew these pictures out of memory; he had remembered her all this time. There were several other sketches but most of it was of hers. She couldn't help but let her tears fall. Worried that she might ruin the papers, she quickly wiped her tears and put all the sheets back in place and into the drawer where it belonged. She couldn't complete any work after that; her thoughts revolved around him and only him. He had always been devoted to her. Those pictures in some way became a proof for his confession of last night— not that she needed it. She had already made a decision, but those sketches helped to solidify it.

Are you free after work? she sent a text message to Roman.

She thought it was better to talk things out with Roman about everything.

He immediately responded, "Yes *Raani*, do you want to go somewhere?"

"Yes, but it is a surprise. I will drive."

They both sat silently inside a car with a mellow music playing in a low volume while Rajmati drove through the winding roads. When he saw the rows of houses stacked like a card in the hill, he realised that they had now reached Kirtipur. They stood on the temple grounds that lay at the highest point in the town.

As they soaked in the view, she exclaimed, "Wow, isn't it beautiful? I love how city looks from here."

"It is," he said looking at her.

When she turned to look at him, his smile faltered ever so slightly. He decided to ask her the question that had been troubling him for a while now, "When I asked, are you happy with this? Why did you say yes?"

Looking down at the ground she replied, "Because that was the answer expected of me."

He nodded and took a long breath.

Then she added, "In a way, I was happy Roman, because it was you. You came in a dark night with a ray of light, and I couldn't help but follow you because you have been my friend. I was not entirely happy because I had just gotten out of a long relationship. I was not willing to get into relationships at all. Our parents' marriages were arranged so I thought, I will just do that and get on with my life."

He kept on looking at her without any words. There was no judgement in his eyes, neither was there any question. He looked at her with no intention to interrupt her so that she could continue saying what she wanted to say. He wanted to hear what she had to say. She then slowly opened up to him about her past and eventually about her breakup.

"I know it was unfair to you to enter into this rebound of a marriage. I would understand if you wanted to end it," she said, looking away from him.

"Have you decided?" he asked her. Not knowing what he meant by that, she looked at him confused.

He then pulled her jacket zipper all the way to the top so that she is prevented from the chilly wind, and asked, his voice almost shaky, "Do you still want to be married to me? I am willing to take all the blame."

She moved slightly away from him, not really understanding what he meant. She said, "I don't know but I know you deserve to be married to someone who loves you. Someone who can return the love you have to give."

"Why are you viewing this relationship as transactional? I am married to the person I am in love with. To love her with all I have is all I ever wanted. I don't want you to feel obligated to love me. It is not about me, trust me on this. If you say you want to stay with me, but you won't love me at all ever, I can survive with the fact alone that you are staying. To be honest, I didn't expect you to, either. The marriage is suddenly thrown at you, like this. I couldn't expect you to fall for me, but one can hope."

"What if I never fall for you," she said unsure if she can commit to what she had just said.

"It's alright," he said not sure if he meant it.

When she looked at him questioningly, he responded, "And if still the question is what am I getting out of it? All I wanted was you, but don't you see even if I wanted you, I would not want to cage you in this relationship. I would not even argue if you decided to leave and take my entire world with you."

"I wouldn't do that," she said adamantly.

116

"But you would my *Raani*, because you are my whole world and if you leave me, I will be someone with no world, just someone lost in space and time."

She could not fathom how someone could love like that. Looking at him now, all she wanted was for him to be happy. She was unsure if it was fair to give him hope of something she might never be able to return. Yet, she also hoped that one day she could love just as deeply as he was capable of loving.

Sometimes the greatest blessing is to be able to love freely and profoundly with only intention is to love and nothing else.

"I don't want to give up. I want to give us a chance," she said. Her words lightened his heart a little, and he instinctively drew her into his arms.

"That's more than enough for me," he whispered.

Chapter 16

It was during Indra Jatra when he saw her crying sitting by the falcha.

"Why are you crying?" Roman had asked her then.

"I really wanted to go see Jatra this year, but Baa has been put if off every time I mention it. I cannot go on my own, he says but he is not taking me to see it either. And I heard that it is the last day of Jatra," she sobbed. *For some reason, his little heart ached to see her cry like that, so he said, "Then I can take you there."*

"Won't we get lost?" she said raising her head a little.

He shook his head no and took her by the hand. As the crowd seemed too big for two schoolkids, he tightened his hold and navigated the crowded road. The loud noise of dhime and Newa bajaa was coming from one end while the cheer of crowd in another. There was a big crowd in the square, looking at Dya pyankha: — a representation of a part of Newa mythology epic in a form of dance. Rajmati and Roman stopped by for a moment looking at the performance in awe then he moved her away from

118

the crowd and to a nearby house which at that time was the highest. He led her by the stairs that took them to the terrace.

"Whose house is this?" she asked curiously.

"It is my grandparents, but the whole place is rented out for shops, but we can access the terrace. From there you can see the entire Jatra with no obstruction. The only issue is you will only get to see the Jatra from above," he huffed as they walked through the stairs.

"Being part of Jatra seems scary as well- too many people. I think having to look at the whole Jatra from above seems even better than not seeing it at all. Thank you so much," she smiled at him. The view was amazing as they hear the beautiful melody from Dhime, jhyali, flute and other instruments followed by Rath, and colourful group of people. She couldn't help but enjoy that time up there. They watched the whole procession from the terrace of Roman's grandparents' house. When they were returning to their homes, they also got to watch Lakhe and Pulukisi visiting houses.

That day she looked ecstatic and happy her smile was wide, and her eyes twinkled in a bright way. She looked most beautiful when she was happy- genuinely happy, Roman thought.

When returning home, they stopped by a shop selling international candies. She asked two of those candies and gave the big one to Roman while saying, "Thank you for today. I loved it so much. Jatra is so fun."

"Is this my payment?" he asked looking at the chocolate.

"I was just being thankful," she responded and pushed the chocolate towards him.

***

Rajmati and Roman were slowly working towards knowing each other and amending things between them. She could see her wall against love slowly chipping off every day that she spent with Roman. As they were not smitten as newlyweds are, people would talk behind their backs assuming their marriage was not working out. Though loveless, it was not miserable as people were making it out to be.

Rajmati was sitting on the chair wearing pyjamas, crossing her legs with notepad in hand and her hair was placed together in a bun with a help of a ball pen while some of her curls had already escaped. She was biting the end of the pencil concentrating hard and looking at the empty notepad when Roman walked into the lounge.

He stopped in his tracks unable to take his eyes off his wife. He then walked towards her putting his hand over her head, he kissed her forehead and whispered, "You look beautiful," making her blush. She wondered how he could possibly find her beautiful when she found herself to be in a messy state. She looked at him not really believing his word, but when her eyes fell on his face, he looked sincere, and he had heart in his eyes. He smiled and walked away picking up his ringing phone.

It was now, she who was looking at the man she had married, busy talking on his phone- authoritative yet polite. His white shirt was neatly folded up to his elbow and his black pants were neatly ironed. He was pacing across the room moving his hands a little, running his hands sometimes over his black hair and after a moment he smiled. She couldn't help but look at that smile and be at awe of it. Then his beautiful amber eyes turned towards her then his smile widened even more brightening his face. Upon realising that she had been staring at him for a little too long, she looked away hastily-

120

darting her eyes here and there and back at him then shyly she looked at the table she was resting her hands at. He approached towards the chair she was sitting at, leaned at the table smirking, he said, "If I was a fool, I would think that my wife was just ogling me."

"Well, I was just appreciating the view," Rajmati's flirting surprised both herself and Roman.

"Well, I am glad you like the view," he recovered but not quite much.

They smiled looking at each other. With their face too close, they didn't know what to say or do. For a moment it felt like they would kiss but the notification on her phone pinged, and the moment passed.

She looked down at her phone scrunching her eyebrows. "What's wrong?" he asked worrying.

"Oh, it's nothing. There is delay in some of the deliveries I requested for the new place we are working on."

The couple went back to their own workplace pretending that nothing had happened but after that moment of being so close to each other, they could not deny that there was some spark, electricity that passed even though it was just for a few seconds.

***

Itumbar was thriving and with the help of new staff members, it was getting much easier to manage the crowd. Her original idea remained intact, and she was more focused to bringing different kinds of game night, musical night to attract patrons to the venue. Slowly things were getting better, things were looking nicer and for the first time she was hopeful. She had considered Roman's advice about hiring a manager so that she could focus on things she wanted to do— to pursue her career in interior designing which would also help with Roman's business. Her fresh and authentic ideas went along with the kind of houses he wanted to sell or buy.

She got caught up with training new manager so much so that she got home really late. She had expected Roman to have gone to sleep but when she reached home, Roman was sitting by the lounge.

"I thought you would be sleeping," she said upon seeing him. The moment he realised that she was back, he rushed towards her.

"Where were you? Why didn't you tell me you were going to be late? Where is your phone?" he asked.

"What do you mean? I texted you that I was going to be late," she said taking her phone out and stumbled upon her next words when she realised that the text was never sent but stayed in the draft along with several missed calls from him, "I am so sorry. I thought I had sent the message, and I also did not realise that my phone was on silent. I am so sorry to worry you like that."

"It's alright, you are home now," he said hugging her. He generally had this cool and calm demeanour but for the first time, she noticed his anxiousness, an undefinable fear in his eyes.

She apologized again, "I am really sorry. I did not realise-"

"It is alright," he said taking one step back. Suddenly his phone started ringing and upon picking up the call, she heard him say, "Yeah, she is here now." Then he thanked the person before putting the phone down.

Confused by the interaction she asked, "Who was it?"

"I was about go to police station, but I thought of making a call to the security personnel at your bar, first and he told me you had just left, so I waited here. It was him calling to make sure that you had arrived," he explained. He then added, "It is not that I don't trust you. I just-"

"Got worried," she completed his sentence and continued, "I am sorry that I made you worry. I will make sure my phone is never on silent. It was late and I was not picking up the call. I understand. I would have done the same because I would have become anxious too if you didn't come home on time."

"You would?" he asked slowly. She only nodded.

"Did you eat?" he asked.

"I didn't get a chance to so I thought I would just heat up something at home. Did you eat?" she asked.

"Nope," he replied sheepishly.

"What? Why haven't you eaten anything? It is so late Roman," she reprimanded him while he stood there listening to her with his arm behind his head. She then pulled him by the arm and took him to the kitchen but stopped in the middle when she saw different pots placed neatly on their dining table.

He then spoke, "I was home early today so I prepared something for both of us. Why don't you go freshen up? I will heat everything up."

"I feel even more guilty now. I am so sorry I came home late when you had done all of this for me," she said feeling terrible. Roman turned her towards him and wrapping her shoulders, he said, "Raani, it is alright. We can still have it together. You did try to contact me, but your phone betrayed you. You go freshen up. Meanwhile, I will reheat them."

She nodded still feeling guilty and moved towards the bedroom to freshen up. By the time she was back, he had already heat up everything for them to feast on. He had made *dyakula*- buffalo meat stew, *aloo tama*- potato and fermented bamboo shoots soup, some green vegetables and rice. As they both sat in the chair, she thanked him and apologized once again. He said, "It is alright. I am glad we can have this dinner together. Now go ahead before it gets cold."

Filling up their plates with all the delicacies that Roman had prepared, the pair started eating.

Just after taking the first bite, Rajmati expressed, "Oh my god! It is so good."

"Food tastes good when one is hungry," he said humbly but she retorted, "No, that's not it. These are really delicious. How did you learn how to make such amazing food."

"I used to spend a lot of time in the kitchen with my mom- I guess, that is how I learned," he said smiling. She nodded with a smile and kept on eating unable to stop herself. He couldn't help but enjoy looking at her savouring the food.

"I am glad you have hired a new manager," he said after a moment.

"I am glad too. She is amazing and fast learner. I might not have to go to bar for much longer," she replied and sipped aloo tama.

"That is good to know. Then, if it is not much of a rush for you, would you like to go to Dolakha, the day after tomorrow with me?"

Chapter 17

How long can you refrain yourself from falling in love? How long will you be able to resist the charm of the next person who loves without any expectations or conditions?

Rajmati and Roman left for Dolakha at the crack of dawn. Both took turns driving the car for the duration of the trip to help the other get rest. They listened to the songs and stole glances at each other occasionally. There was a comfort in the silence and melodious music in the background. They would share some titbits of their life or talk about their favourite songs. After 3 hours on the road, they stopped by to grab something to eat and in another 3 hours, they were in Dolakha. They went straight to their lodge to eat and rest. Next day, they were up and ready for the work they were there for— to meet up with local council regarding their business setup.

The locals were rather sceptical and worried that if such development might destroy their much-preserved cultural heritage. Roman, however, had no such intention. He wanted to open an accommodation service for tourists. He did not want to change anything in the place, instead, he wanted to showcase the culture of the place and wanted to learn more about it to incorporate its intricate detail in his venture, so that the guests can feel comfortable and experience the beauty of the location. He wanted to ensure that locals would get the job, and the local businesses would flourish with his approach. They were also there to impart this message to the local and give them assurance that this development would not hinder their growth or challenge the preservation of the cultural heritage.

Roman rubbed his hand blowing warm air in his hand. The weather was colder there than it was in Kathmandu, probably because it was more in the elevated side of the country. Rajmati took out an extra glove she had kept in her pocket and taking his hand in hers, she put those gloves in his hand.

Seeing the surprise in his eyes, she responded, "Well, I took it out for you to wear but you forgot so I put it in my pocket."

"Good to know that you do care about me," he teased her.

"Of course, I do, when have I ever said that I don't," she held her ground and he couldn't help but look at her in awe. She blushed and looked away continuing to walk along the path.

They were roaming around the place and visiting different abandoned houses in the area. There were many houses that were abandoned because there were no longer families living in the house. While most families moved abroad, many decided to settle in the city area. While some were willing to sell their properties, some wanted to hold onto their ancestral land and house but could not come and live in it. Roman offered to get those kinds of properties on lease or on rent.

"I cannot believe people no longer live in these beautiful houses," she said admiringly looking at the street that consisted of almost similar looking beautiful cottage like houses with ornate crafted wooden windows and small sitting area at the front.

"So, I don't get it, you are renting the place and also upscaling it?" Rajmati asked not really understanding the strategy.

"I am renting the place but most of the plumbing and reparation must be done by the owner before I take over. Then interior, where you come in, will be done as per our wish. We just have to make sure it is renter-friendly because of the contract we have with them."

"Ahh, ok, that's interesting. And people agreed to it?"

"Some of them did and some of them didn't. Luckily, all these ten houses' owners agreed and is ready for us. Investors are also happy with the location. We will set up an office in the area for administration purposes," Roman said while Rajmati already had ideas churning in her mind to make this place look authentic and homely.

"How about staff members?" she asked.

"We will be hiring local youths from the area as they would know more about the local community and are looking for job as well."

"Will people come all the way here?" Rajmati asked.

"Bhimshenthan temple is one of the popular temples here that attracts lots of visitors and another is Kalinchok temple a little further away from here. I heard it is going to be another destination for people to enjoy snow in winter."

"Wow will there be snowfall?" she asked excitedly.

"Are you kids going to destroy all these houses?" asked one old lady before he could answer Rajmati.

"No, no, *aama,* we are not doing such things," Roman explained, "we are only renting this place so that visitors can come and stay. The originality and the essence of these places will not be affected."

"These are our identity. I hope you don't destroy this," she said with concern.

"If anything, we will only uplift it and preserve its heritage," Rajmati reassured.

The old lady nodded and left after saying, "If that's the case, I hope you both succeed. My blessings are with you."

Later in the afternoon, they met the local council and the head of community to discuss about the plan, administration, strategy, to share their development ideas and to address the concerns that community might have. It was not an easy conversation at first and required lots of convincing and assurance. Eventually, they were happy about the idea Roman had and when Rajmati expressed her idea of interior and promotion of local food, they were delighted. They felt at ease to know that they had good intention indeed. They were even happier to know that these houses would not be as abandoned as it were now.

They were walking along the stone paved road— elated after the response of the council when another old lady came in front of them asking, "Are you two here for a honeymoon?"

"We are actually here for work," Roman replied.

"Ahh, all work is no fun. I thought you couples were here for the Bhim Ekadashi Puja happening in Bhimshenthan, today. People from all around the places come to celebrate this day. If you have time, you should come as well. Don't miss out as you are already here," the old lady suggested.

"Sure, we will be there. When is it?" Rajmati responded.

"The main part will start around evening today. The gathering would start soon now. You can join whenever you feel like. See you there, then," said the lady and moved along waving someone in the distant.

There was a huge crowd of people surrounding the temple when Roman and Rajmati reached there. Everyone was holding various kinds of *diyo*, an oil lamp to offer it to the God and around the temple. The night sky was dark, but the ground was lit up. They roamed around the temple, worshiped and offered fruits and oil lamp. It was meditative to watch the procession of people with different instruments and rituals going on around them. While crowd disseminated, they held onto their hands even when the earlier excuse of not wanting to get lost in crowd had long gone.

After their visit to the Bhimsenthan, they had dinner at a local restaurant and before returning to their lodge, they decided to walk around a little. The stars were bright and shining in the sky; it was unlike what you see in the city amidst all the light pollution. They were awestruck by the beauty they witnessed from this hilly area— for a moment there, they were lost in time and space.

Roman then turned towards Rajmati and asked, "Do you want to go and see snow tomorrow before we leave?"

"Are you serious?" she exclaimed in surprise.

"Yes, I thought because winter is almost over, there would not be much snow, but I heard from the locals that there could be snowfall over the hill near Kalinchok. If you want to go, we can," he responded.

"I would love to," she said bringing her palms together in excitement.

***

Next morning they went to upper hill side of the village and just like the locals suggested, the hill was now all white, covered in snow patches with snowflakes still gently falling from the sky. Her excitement was clear in her face which led Roman to ask, "Is this your first snow?"

"Yes, and it is so lovely. Thank you so much," she said extending her hands to catch the falling snow.

"It is indeed. Let me get some photos of you," he said taking out his phone from his jacket pocket.

She laughed at first then she struck a pose by throwing snow in the air while he took lots of pictures to remember this day by.

"Ok, enough of my photos, let's take yours," she said moving towards him.

"Let's take a selfie instead," he suggested. Then, he turned away, extended his hand with phone towards the sky while she made heart with her fingers bringing her face close to his, breathing the same air, both eyes looking at the camera. Snap. As he lowered his hand, both turned their heads to one another, their lips almost touching, their breath appearing as vapor in the cold air. Before she could look away, her feet slipped, and his arms grabbed her by the waist preventing her fall. Both straightened up quickly, his eyes searching to make sure she is alright and her eyes reassuring that she is. Then both their eyes lingered a little more in each other's lips.

A moment passed and they moved away from each other. Before he could walk away, she pulled him by the arm and before either of them realised what was happening her lips were on his. She did not know if it was the snow, long drive they took, the conversations they shared, all the recent moments or just this moment that made her kiss him, but she could no longer ignore the feeling that was growing for him within her heart.

"I love you," she whispered. With mountains in the backdrop, holding onto each other, she confessed her love for him for the first time in all these months. It might have been his attentiveness, his protectiveness and most of all his willingness to love her without any expectation of that love to be returned that she could no longer pretend that his presence did not affect her. She could no longer cage her heart and stop

132

it from loving the person who would bestow his world for her. She needed to tell him her feelings and at that moment when they kissed, her feelings felt more than real, and it became important to let him know how she felt about him. Thats what love is perhaps, it finds its way to worm in because a person's heart wants to love as much as it longs for love.

Roman who was already surprised by the kiss was now stunned by what he had just heard. He almost did not believe if he heard her correctly. The snow fell over them as they stared into each other's eyes. The wind was blowing slightly. In that freezing weather, one could not tell if their faces were turning red because of the cold, or from blushing.

His mouth opened and closed, not knowing what he should say next then somehow, some words escaped like a breath from his mouth, "Raani, you are not going to take it back, are you?"

She held his face with her palms and looking into his eyes, she expressed, this time more confidently, "I love you Roman. I would never retract these words. Thank you for giving us a chance and letting me stay. Thank you for your patience. Thank you for freeing my heart and letting it come to you. I am sorry, it took me so long. I plan on loving you and keep on loving if you allow me to- unless you've changed your min-"

"I love you Raani, so much," he said interrupting her blabber and pulled her into yet another kiss.

They end up staying another night in Dolakha and just like the old lady suggested, it did sort of become their honeymoon.

Chapter 18

They say that love finds its way even in the challenging time. Even when one may think they cannot win over, Love makes it way to you. Matina, Maya, Love— so many names, so many meanings to that one word. The weight it carries, the emotions one feels around that one person with that one word is tremendous.

Something shifted in the air that night- it felt like love and blessings. The expression of love, acceptance of it, does something to a person's soul- it rejoices, takes a flight somewhere and the world feels like it has slowed down. They were more in each other's arm than not. Roman did not want to let her go anywhere while she didn't mind snuggling next to him. It was almost like the world paused for them.

When they were back in Kathmandu, their hearts were more lightened and face happier. The people in the world did not have to acknowledge or validate their happiness. They were happy and that was all that mattered.

"Something's changed," Charu said from the other end of the phone call. Rajmati was preparing dinner and talking to Charu via her headphones, leaving her phone on the kitchen counter.

"What do you mean?" Rajmati asked her friend not quite understanding her.

"Your voice. It sounds different. Something has changed. What happened? You have got to spill," Charu said excitedly.

"I- I don't know what you are talking about," Rajmati chuckled.

"See, you are laughing and smiling. You sound happy and I am so happy to hear that voice after so long. He is treating you well, Mati, am I right?" Charu asked- her happiness for her friend exuding through her voice.

"Yes," Rajmati responded slowly.

"I knew it. You are finally in love with your husband," Charu teased her.

"Oh, shut up" Rajmati said and before she could say anything more, she shrieked in pain.

"Hey, what happened?" Charu asked with concern.

"Oh no, it's nothing. I nicked my fingers while cutting the onions and its bleeding all over the counter. Sorry I will call you back. I have to get the band aid."

"Oh no, you should be paying attention. Put on the band aid and call me back. Take care."

***

"Raani," Roman called out from the other room, but when he did not hear any response, he walked towards the kitchen looking for her. He instead noticed small droplets of blood on the floor and on the kitchen counter. Suddenly, his heartbeat raced, and his concern swelled up further leading him to frantically search for her, "Raani," he screamed and went inside the pantry then to the bathroom only to find her sitting by the bathtub. She was calmly going through the first aid box elevating her left hand that had a small cut and a blood slightly oozing out. Her emotions stark opposite from his.

"Why didn't you call me?" he asked making her startle.

"Oh, it was just the small cut, so I just thought I would get a band aid," she explained continuing her search for band aid in the box with one hand while he moved towards her.

"But why didn't you ask me to come and help you with this?" he asked again, taking the first aid box from her hand. He then took out a bottle and a band aid from the box before putting it aside.

"It is not a big deal Roman, nothing I can't handle. Anyways, you were working," she responded and extended her hand to take the band aid from him, but he moved towards her and held her left hand instead and examined the cut.

"You should. I am never too busy for you. You don't have to do it alone," he said and meant every word of it.

Before putting the disinfectant, he warned her, "this might sting."

136

She hissed a little in pain and said, "All I needed was a band aid."

"It is good to disinfect cut before putting on the band aid," he said and wrapped her slender finger with a band aid. She slowly brought her hand down and looking up at him she whispered, "Thank you."

Then kneeling in front of her, he asked, "Raani, next time no matter what happens, you will ask for the help if you need one, right?"

"Where is this coming from? It was just a small cut, Ro."

"It does not matter how small or big things are, you would come to me, won't you?" he asked. He needed the assurance that she would not worry over things by herself when he could help or at least listen to her. He did not want to miss out on the signs.

***

Rajmati went silent over his request. For someone who had to do things on her own and figure things out for so long that she no longer knew how to ask for help. He kept on looking at her while she looked at her injury in silence. When she looked back at him, she saw the swirling of emotions in his eyes which she could not fathom so she asked, "Ro, are you ok?"

But he just stood up and walked towards the room, pacing around. His eyes were scared; his heartbeats were racing. She didn't know what to do so she went ahead and hugged him. Slowly, he calmed down, hugged her back and both stayed still in the moment. He then kissed her forehead and said, "Thank you."

She didn't know if she should ask him what had just happened. He did not further explain either but before she could walk away, he held her hands and asked again, "You will let me know if you need anything, or if anything is bothering you, anything at all, right?"

She sighed upon his request and said, "I am not used to asking for help Roman. I can do things on my own. I cannot come to you for every little thing."

"But of course you can, Raani. I would do anything for you. Please promise me, you would tell me if anything were bothering you or if you need help or if you need to talk. Please," his voice was scattered and sounded rather breathless which startled Rajmati all over again.

She held his hands and said, "I will Roman. I will try my best to not shy away from asking for a help but please understand it is not an easy thing for me because I never had to. I am used to doing things on my own."

"I understand. I will try to learn your needs before you can even ask for it, but please understand, you don't have to things on your own all the time. You can share your burden with me," he said bringing his hands to her face and pulling her into a kiss.

She was appreciative of what he said and grateful to have someone like him as her partner but at the same time she could not help but notice the anxiety that she had seen in his eyes. It was different and she could not fathom the reason behind it.

Many times, he had woken up scared and lost. She had started to take notice of how at times he became extremely overprotective not of the men looking at her but seeing her lost in thoughts, or when she is depressed or frustrated at a very minute thing. It was never a mistrust that she saw in his eyes, but it was a fear that prevailed. The reason behind the fear however, she still could not comprehend. The mood shifted the moment she is not smiling or talking. It was endearing to receive such care and attention but such level of observation, was it healthy? Was there something going on his mind that he had not yet shared with her? What demons were eating him so much that he could not help but be concerned all the time?

Chapter 19

The air was bone-chillingly cold, and people could be seen holding onto their warm cup of tea for a little longer to savour the warmth it exuded. With winter festivals approaching and Maha Shivaratri just around the corner, the valley had seen the gradual increase of Sadhus and Hindu pilgrims from all over the world, each arriving to celebrate the occasion.

In the similarly cold Saturday morning, Rajmati was meeting her friends at the newly opened restaurant. Tara was invited by the restaurant owner so that she could talk about it in her social media and in her newsletters. The restaurant had a modern chic look with black and white theme. However, the dishes served were rather colourful, creating a distinct contrast that emphasised the fact that the only thing of importance was the food and to relish it. And for being a restaurant that served fusion Mexican Nepali food, the delicacies looked equally tasteful.

They were sitting around a small circular table situated in a corner. There also was an electric heater placed near them to

140

help combat the cold. As three friends ordered their food, they immediately jumped into the conversation. Charu had already filled in Tara about Rajmati's recent confession of love to her husband as soon as she had found out about it.

"I did not expect you to fall for Roman this soon, to be honest," Tara said while diligently snapping pictures around the venue.

"I could not help it. He is so patient and understanding," Rajmati responded.

"That is nice to hear but I have to ask this is not you wanting to love someone because your heart feels empty, right?" Tara asked.

"What are you, a therapist?" Rajmati responded jokingly and slightly taken aback by her question, unsure if she had the right answer to that question. When both her friends looked at her for an answer to Tara's question, she sighed and said, "Tara, weren't you the one who said, I should not refrain myself from such beautiful feelings and that I should not give more power to that person who never understood my value?"

"Umm, I posed it more like a question than a statement that you are making it out to be," Tara prompted.

"We just want to make sure that you are not rushing this," Charu said next.

"It is not just a rebound, okay? If that's what you are thinking," Rajmati said exasperated and continued, "Me and Nhugha were done a long time ago. We were barely hanging on. Was I sad when we broke up? Yes, because it was the longest relationship I had ever been in. I realised that it was a sinking ship too late, and he had already jumped out of it while leaving me to drown. It was not a worthy relationship to cry over or to stop myself from giving another chance at love."

"That is so good to know. We are happy for you and Roman, truly but we just wanted to make sure that you said that you love him because you meant it and not because you feel obligated to return his feelings or thought that was the only way to make things right."

"Aren't you guys the ones who told me to give this a chance?"

"Not with a 'I love you' thrown in the mix so soon," Tara exclaimed.

Charu on the other hand, calmly said, "Last time we chatted, you didn't seem to be ready for the relationship or even being with him, so we were just concerned that your heart is in the right place. I know we are the one who told you to move on, but we also realise that moving on takes time and you are allowed to do that if that's what you need. We don't want to see either of you getting hurt."

"Charu, I understand but I really do love him," Rajmati expressed.

"Ok, ok we believe you," Charu said smiling not wanting to stretch this any further.

"So, tell us how he is like. What got you so smitten with him?" Tara asked next finally putting the phone down and resting elbows on the table, she gave her full attention to her friends.

Rajmati blushed a little and began, "Well, he is helpful, listens to me, cooks really good food and I absolutely adore how he can look absolutely serious and cute at the same time."

"All the valid reason to be smitten," Tara said, and Charu agreed.

Then, Tara asked, "He seems like a guy who cares a lot about you."

"Yeah, sometimes a little too much," Rajmati muttered.

"What is that supposed to mean?" Charu asked.

"I don't know. He is just too observant, at times."

"Are you bragging?" Tara teased her making Rajmati laugh.

"No. Not at all. I just worry if there is something else that is bothering him," Rajmati said.

"I suppose that's a good thing. I mean how many men are observant these days," Tara shrugged.

"Tuyucha was never observant enough to be honest, so you have accepted bare minimum to be the benchmark," Charu said.

"I know. Maybe I am just not used to it, I guess," Rajmati sighed. His perceptive nature had been somewhat confusing to her recently. She was not sure if it was, she who was not used to such gesture or if it was, he who had a lot going on his mind and was not sharing enough.

Rajmati cleared her throat and looking at her friends, she said, "Ok, can I ask you this? There can be a comfortable

143

silence, can't there? People can be lost in thoughts. But even when I am staring at the ceiling thinking of the next project, he gets all worried and keeps on asking if everything is alright. Is that normal? I mean, I appreciate the gesture. I love it even, but he seems to be constantly on edge."

A young lady brought their drinks and placed it in front of them with a smile. All of them nodded and thanked her, pausing their conversation in the middle. Then Tara took out her phone and took photos of their beverages.

"Still feels like bragging to me," Tara joked then added, "But to answer your question, maybe he really is just concerned about you. Since it's all new to you, he might only want to make sure you feel comfortable. That's a good thing, my dearest friend," Tara assured her, carefully angling her phone to snap another picture of their drinks.

"Maybe you are right," Rajmati said sceptically.

"Let's be honest, you don't really ask for help so maybe he is just trying to make sure that you know he is available if you need anything. It is ok to ask for help, love," Charu said this time after taking a sip of her honey ginger lemon tea.

"He also said the same thing. He was rather insistent about it as well. Maybe you are right. I am just overthinking. Anyways, enough about me, let's talk about what is happening in your life?" Rajmati said to her friends picking up her cup to drink the tea.

"Well, this is my recent project," Tara said showing the restaurant.

144

"And it's amazing. Thank you for inviting us to this lovely place," Rajmati said, appreciating the restaurant where they were having lunch. Then, Charu added, "We hope you get invited to such projects more often, so we get to enjoy the fruits of your hard work," which made all of them laugh. After a moment, Charu cleared her throat and, looking at her friends expectantly, said, "I have something to tell you guys." Both friends turned to her with interest as she said almost in a one breath, "I'm finally having my art exhibition."

"Are you kidding? That should have been the first thing you told us. Congratulations! Oh my gosh! this is so exciting," Rajmati said hugging Charu.

Tara looking equally excited, stood up to hug and congratulate her, then she added, "Where is it going to happen? I am so happy for you."

"It is going to be at the Mul Chowk in Patan Durbar Square in couple of months. I am so excited too and both of you must come, okay?" Charu said mixing her excitement with her friends.

"Of course we will. I am so happy for you," Rajmati said with her eyes full of pride and joy for her friend.

After spending the whole afternoon together, the trio decided to head home. Before Rajmati could do so, however, she received a call from her bar manager about an issue in the brewing area. She dropped both her friends off at their homes and made her way to the bar. On the way, she noticed her car was making spluttering noises but decided to look into it later and headed inside.

***

The place was crowded as usual and after greeting few of the regular customer she had known and her staff members, she went to talk to the manager, Sharon, who then took her to the brewing area. Sharon did not want to take any action before showing it to Rajmati as the brewing station was traditionally built and pretty old as well.

Rajmati noticed that one of the pipes was leaking and made a mess around the whole station. She quickly made a call to the local repairer who had been coming to fix any issues they had in the bar since a long time ago. She then asked Sharon to call cleaner immediately to which Sharon replied that she had already done that. After that Rajmati went to close the knob and tried to inspect the pipe as per the advice of the repairer. It seemed that the pipe had gotten old and needed a replacement so she texted the repairer about it so that he could bring the things he would need for it.

She walked with Sharon around the bar and addressed any pending and accounting issues. After some time, the repairer came and fixed the pipes. By the time everything was done, it was already late, and bar was starting to get quieter. The serious issues were fixed and for some remaining concerns, she decided to handle them in few days.

She looked around the space— empty bar and silence it prevailed; she was lost in thoughts of how far she had come and how things have changed. She reminisced a little and taking a long sigh of relief after the hectic evening, she walked towards the door but before she could even reach the main door, she heard an excruciating noise making her turn back to find the source. She saw that the whole glass cabinet behind the bar had collapsed. When she reached the bar area, it was all shards of glass on the floor and most of alcohol bottles dispensed along with it. It seemed that the glass base could no longer handle the pressure, so it came apart. Though tired, she picked up the large broom and cleared up the area. She put in a mental note to call cabinetmaker to fix it. As it was only side of the cabinet, she decided to take out all the other alcohols from the other side so that the same fate would not occur again. At that point, she also decided to change the glass base to steel one and change the style of cabinet to have more wooden and steel look. When she put the last bottle down in a bottom cabinet, she thanked her goddess that it happened at night and not when people were working around this area. She texted Sharon about the incident and advised her to be careful. Then before she could leave, she noticed that one of the *ailah* bottle had survived the fall and found refuge under the crook of a cabinet. It was the bottle that was sealed when she first helped her father brew *ailah*. It was never opened, and she was glad that it was not shattered, so she took it from the ground, inspected the bottle, wiped off the dust and put it in her bag. She finally closed the venue for the night and walked towards her car but when she tried to start her car, it just spluttered and did not budge. She had had enough of it. The evening just had gotten worse by the second. It was late at night, and she was not sure if any mechanic would be available. She could leave the car here and take a taxi home, but it would be hard to find the taxi at that hour. She thought of going upstairs of the bar to her parents' place, but her parents were in Sankhu, visiting family for a week and she did not have the keys with her.

"You can ask for help you know," Charu's voice resonated.

"You will tell me if you need anything right?" Roman's voice came next in her mind. She was not used to asking for help. She had never done that before, and she did not know how until now. Before she could dwell more in the dilemma, her

hand on its own accord made a call to Roman. She at first thought, she would only call him to inform him that she will be further late but the moment he said, "Yes, Raani," she broke down and said, "I am so tired. My car broke down. It has been one thing after another." She continued with the saga of her evening at the bar and ended it with, "And I am stranded in front my bar."

He did not interrupt the entire time and listened to her patiently and once she stopped, he said, "I am almost there Raani. Please stay where you are. Just few more minutes." Rajmati was surprised to hear that he was already on his way. All this time when she was talking, he was on his way there.

Just like he promised, he arrived within few minutes. He hurriedly parked the car and walked towards her.

She was used to doing things on her own but that day talking to him about her day, the frustration it held and him rushing to her upon just a call, made her feel like a heavy burden was lifted off of her— as if his presence alone was able to make everything right and made her feel light melting all her stress away. She ran into his arms without any second thought, and he held her without any questions asked. They stayed like that for a while and after all this time spent on earth, Rajmati for the first time felt what it was like to rely on someone and for that someone to be there for her.

He then looked at her and while checking her hand and face, he asked, "Are you alright? You are not hurt, are you?"

She only moved her head to say no, then he pulled her into a hug again caressing her hair as she relaxed in his arms.

***

148

Later that night, when they reached home, she stopped him by his arms and asked, "Would you like to have a drink with me?"

He turned to look at her, surprise evident in his face.

She then added, "When all the bottles shattered, some of them remained intact." Then she opened her bag and took out an old glass bottle sealed with muslin cloth covered cork, and continued, "This was one of those bottles, this was sealed when I first brewed alcohol with my dad. Do you want to share a shot of this drink with me."

"Wouldn't you want to share it with your dad?" he asked.

"I will send the bottle home but the first drink, I would like to have it with you after this mess of a night."

"I would love to," he smiled looking at his wife with eyes full of love.

"Cheers" they said and gulped down the shot of *ailah*. The spirit washed down their throat burning it along the way.

"That's good," he expressed in his hoarse voice induced by the ailah.

She only nodded and then both smiled at each other.

"Would you like to go to Charu's exhibition with me?" she blurted out of nowhere.

"Wow, is she having an exhibition? That is great. I would love to. Just tell me when and where?" he said.

She put the information on his phone and handed it over. Then their hands lingered over one another, soon enough their hands found each other's face and their lips collided in passion.

All her former concerns about his perceptive nature were slowly clearing away.

Could she have been just seeing things because she just did not want to believe that someone could care for her?

Chapter 20

Whether it was small or big things, he would never hesitate to be there for her.

"Are you still worried?" he would ask.

"No, I am not. Not anymore." She would reply.

A silly argument here and there, a few longing glances, finding beauty in the mundane and finding oneself in the new phase of life, Rajmati and Roman slowly found their footing in their marriage and every day slowly and steadily fell increasingly in love with each other. It was almost a year since their wedding. This time they celebrated Yomari Punhi with both their families and Matina Paaru was more exciting than the last one.

She had been more actively pursuing her career in interior designing and had opened her own firm with clients ranging from commercial and influential people to residential and cause driven projects. Rajmati and Roman were doing well together with both helping each other in their business. The society that had known Rajmati since young refused to talk about it—about how their dynamic was powerful. As much as she loved being her own girl with her own company that she ran proudly, she also loved coming home to him and sharing everything about the day she just had. He would sit there and listen to her with all his attention. Roman rarely shared what was happening with him though. He would tell her about the in and out of his work but rarely he shared the in and out of his mind.

There would be at times she would find Roman rather anxious, and she wanted to help him navigate it. She wanted to be there for him like he was there for her, but he never shared his nightmares with her, and he would always wave it off as a bad dream but some part for her knew that there was something that bothered him. She was yet to navigate that side of their relationship and was hopeful he will share what kept him at night when he was ready.

As their anniversary was approaching, Roman asked her, "Would you like to spend our anniversary in Sydney instead? It will be summer there and perfect to spend time in the beach."

"That sounds good," she responded.

***

They were driving across the coastal road with some popular song playing in the car. They were not paying much attention to the song on the radio as much as they were enjoying the view and their conversation. The blue sky with fairy floss clouds above and cool blue ocean below while they

152

drove across the road was majestic and peaceful. Rajmati looked at the view and exclaimed, "It is so beautiful."

Roman moved his head slightly away from the road and relished the view a little and brought his head back to the road agreeing with her, "Wait till you see the beach I am about to take you to."

"But the sun is about to set, will we get there on time?"

"Oh, there is plenty of time for the sun to set and that place is even beautiful at night," he replied.

After driving further for an hour and a half, they finally reached the beach Roman was raving about- Hyams Beach in Jervis Bay. They put their picnic blanket on the white sand overlooking the vast bay and greens surrounding them.

"Me and my Uni friends used to come here," Roman said lying on the blanket.

"Did you have lots of friends here?" she asked.

"Not many but enough to count on them when I needed them. We did so many fun, spontaneous thing, the perks of being young and wild I guess," he laughed while reminiscing his days in Sydney.

"That sounds nice. You are so lucky to have such a group of friends in a foreign country. Are they also back in Nepal?"

"No, they are in different parts of Australia now. Some of them are coming to meet us this time. I will introduce you to them this week."

"That sounds great. I would love to meet them. I rarely meet your friends— if your corporate 'friends' can be counted as friends," she joked, and he laughed.

"Well, that's because my friends are scattered around the globe," he responded and after a moment while looking far into the horizon, he said, "You know, this city and the friends I met here taught me lots of life skills. I am so grateful of this."

"Tell me more," she said turning towards him and he looked at her not really understanding her, so she explained, "Tell me more about your life here, your friends. I love it when you show me the glimpse of your past. Did you have any exes I should know about?"

He chuckled a little and spoke, "No, not really. I did date in the past, but I knew my heart was not in it."

"Was it plural?"

"Am I in trouble, if it is?"

"No, not really, we all have our past." They laughed again and looked away.

"My first job here was as server and kitchen hand in a tiny Indian restaurant," he said, "I met a girl there and she seemed fun, and I think she was only looking for fun as well. We hooked up but nothing happened between us."

"Was it tough working in a restaurant?" she asked ignoring the fact that he talked about a girl.

"So, we are not going to talk about the girl I dated," he stated to which she chuckled and said, "No, we are not, unless you want to talk about her."

"Nah, I don't want to. The only person I ever want to talk about is you," he said making her blush and added, "and yes, it was tough but like every job I did in my life, I have acquired skills from each of them, so I am glad to have done various kinds of jobs in my life. It made me who I am today. I didn't mean to sound it like I am giving a job interview but that's true."

"That is so cool. The only job I ever did was bartending."

"Which is tough in its own right— you also meet different kinds of people there so you must have learned a lot about people skills from there."

"Yeah, I did. Now it really is starting to sound like two people talking in a career expo," she joked.

"Agreed," he said raising his both hands in defeat.

"I am so glad you had people to look up and go to despite being away from home," she said after a moment.

"Thank you. I am also glad you always had your two best friends with you- always supporting one another. Friends you make when you were little and growing up are quite special, isn't it?" he said with some melancholy in his eyes.

"Yeah, I am lucky to have them around in my life. From gossips to life goals, it is great to have them though we tend to annoy each other at times," she laughed, and he joined her.

Continuing their talk, she asked, "How about your school friends? Are you still in touch with them? How about that boy you always flew kite with or seemed always to be playing around with? Do you still see him time to time? Or is he also abroad?"

"No," he said abruptly surprising her and then went silent. One word answer for all the questions she had asked. No— one word that was so raw and straightforward that she was not sure if she should ask him more about it or say nothing at all. Just like that the wall they had tumbled down seemed to have come back again.

"Do you want some ice cream?" he asked interrupting her train of thoughts and before she could say anything, he got up and walked towards an ice cream van leaving her baffled. She wondered if there was rift between him and his friend. She decided not to bring it up unless he did.

He came back after a while with two ice-creams and a smile in his face. Maybe it was not a big of a deal. Some friends drift apart, and people do not talk about them. Maybe it was just a plain, simple No- *"No, I don't have any school friends."* He did have to leave the valley when he was still in school, so he may not have been able to be in touch with his friends as much. She smiled back saying, "Thank you," and took one of the ice-creams from him.

They sat there looking at the vast waterbody and sky changing its colour— in that moment, they found peace momentarily. Slowly as the sun disappeared from the sky and stars made its way, the oceanic bay somehow came alive with fluorescent shades of colour shining through the water. The view was breathtaking, so much so that Rajmati stared at scene in front of her speechless, while Roman looked at her with the same awe.

"It is bioluminescence. I have heard it is a rare occurrence that is why I didn't tell you before because I was not sure if it would appear. We must be lucky tonight to be able to see this phenomenon."

"Wow, it is so beautiful. Thank you so much for bringing me here," she said unable to hide the awe in her voice. She put her head over his shoulders and relished the night view as it unfolded. That night they stayed in a nearby hotel.

During their visit, they did lots of exciting things, met his friends, visited different places and out of all the nights that they spent there, both Rajmati and Roman would say that the night they spent talking under the starlight watching ocean and sky come alive was the best of all the nights. It might have been the view that graced them or the way Roman slowly opened to her about his friends and his life in Sydney along the ride and the beach. Though there was a moment when it felt like he was not telling her everything, but it still was more than what he usually shared.

***

After celebrating their anniversary week in Sydney, Roman and Rajmati were at their work and busier than ever. Roman was on his never-ending phone calls while Rajmati was working on her new project in her tablet, when her phone started buzzing and to her surprise it was Kavya who was calling her.

"Jojolapa, Rajmati Ji, how are you?" he greeted her as she picked up his call.

"Jojolapa Kabiji, what a pleasant surprise," she said and as soon as she said that Roman turned around looking curiously towards her while he still listening to the person on the phone.

It had been about six months since Rajmati had last met Kavya at Charu's exhibition. She was pleasantly surprised to learn that he had played a pivotal role in helping Charu connect with the organiser and bring the event to life. The exhibition turned out to be a success and Rajmati couldn't help but feel proud as she watched her friends' artwork displayed and admired my many. Little did any of them knew, that the very event would mark the beginning of Charu's journey as an established artist and propel her to the next level.

That exhibition was also the day that Roman and Kavya got a chance to talk to each other. It was then when Roman learned that Kavya was dedicating a ballad for Rajmati in his upcoming book. There was a certain unknown emotion that passed in his eyes upon getting that information.

When she put the phone down, Roman also cut his call short and walked towards her asking what it was about failing terribly at hiding his curiosity. Ever since he met Kavya at Charu's exhibition, Roman had been rather interested about Kavya's intentions.

"It is nothing," she said almost smiling at her husband's eagerness. She continued, "He was just saying that the book was finished and will have it deliver to us."

"Is he going to come here?" he asked trying to sound nonchalant.

"No— I mean, I didn't ask. I assumed he will have someone deliver it to our place," she said her voice now slowly rising with realisation, "Did I just ask a poet to come and deliver his book to the house. Oh, no, that is so embarrassing. I should have offered to pick it up, right?"

"Maybe he is getting it delivered by someone," he tried to reassure her, but she was already pacing around.

"Raani, it is not a big of a deal," Roman huffed.

Chapter 21

It was warm Saturday morning and rays of sun were making its way to her room. Roman and Rajmati had hired a housekeeper, Rupa, to help around the house every Saturday. She was a young diligent girl in her late teens working part time as housekeeper to save money for her tuition fees.

While Rupa was cleaning downstairs, Rajmati was upstairs arranging her closet. She was finally getting a chance to rearrange and declutter her closet, the task that she had been putting off for a long time. Her clothes were strewn on the floor, and she was surrounded by small cardboard boxes. She was going through her jewellery box when she found her *bizakani*. It was her favourite piece of jewellery once upon a time- so much so that she would always be found wearing it. She had found it in a vintage shop and having never seen such earrings before; she was enraptured by it. When the shopkeeper said that it was *bizakani*, one of the traditional ornaments that was no longer made, she believed it to be so.

She now had one left with her because its other pair was lost from her. It had been a long time since she saw it or even missed it so she decided to part ways with it and put it in a pile of giveaways but before she could do that, a bell rang, and she got up to go downstairs putting the earring in her pocket instead. Rupa must have opened the doors by the time she got to the stairs, tying her hair in a bun. Kavya was looking at her from downstairs wearing his beige coat and pants holding a book in his hand.

He had mentioned that the book will be delivered to her place but just like she guessed it was the poet himself who was delivering the said book. She felt a little bad for not realising that she had not even offered to pick it up and instead asked him to deliver it.

"*Jojolapa* Kabiji, how are you doing? It is so nice to see you," Rajmati said from the top of the stairs. He did not speak for a moment while she walked down the stairs and by the time she reached the bottom of the stairs, he said, "It is so good to see you too. You are just as beautiful as always if not more. How are you?"

Rajmati blushed a little at the compliment and appreciated his kind words but humbly brushed it away. They chatted a little but realising that she hadn't even offered him any food, she went inside the kitchen to get him some tea and snacks but to her surprise Rupa had already prepared the tea and was about to set up the tray.

"Thank you so much, Rupa," Rajmati said taking out two packets of Tim Tam from the cabinet.

"Ma'am, I have to leave early today," Rupa said and continued, "I had already told Sir, but he seemed to have left."

161

"I know, he has already told me that you need to take your son to the clinic. It is alright. Take care and let me know if you need any help alright?" Rajmati said reassuringly.

"Thank you for understanding," she replied and handed Rupa a bag consisting of packet of chocolates, a small handbag and while adding another packet of Tim Tam she said, "This is for your son, and this is a small bag that I got for you from Sydney. I hope you like it."

"Oh, that is so nice of you. You didn't have to but thank you so much," Rupa said elated and left with a smile in her face.

Later she brought tea and snacks to Kavya, and they got immersed in their conversation. She was flattered and overwhelmed seeing the book with her name on it. She was curious to learn what had been written but she was unsure if she wanted to meet the girl she had left behind a long time ago.

He suddenly asked her, "Are you happy?" which caught her off guard. She could not understand where this question was coming from. Did she not look happy? She certainly felt happy, so she just responded by a nod and a smile. She then added, "Yes, I am. Thank you for asking."

There was not really a reason not to be except for her concern around Roman's anxiousness but that was not something Kabiji needed to know. She didn't know if he believed the answer she gave to him, but it was not a lie. She was indeed happy to be with such an amazing and loving husband.

After a moment, Kavya proceeded to take something out of his pocket. It was another pair of Bizakani that she had thought she had lost. She did not remember where she had lost it and had forgotten all about it until a moment ago when she found the other pair. When he extended his hand to give it to her, she refused and said, "It's alright, I do not want it. I want things from my past to remain in past. If you don't mind, please keep it as a thank you for naming a book after me. You can give it away if you prefer."

He hesitated a little and looking at the Bizakani in his hand, he said, "Are you really sure about this? I thought it would be something that would be part of you as you would always be seen wearing it."

"It is a piece of jewellery- not a part of me. It does not really represent me either. I lost my attachment to it the day I lost it. In fact, here is another, earring of it to make a pair, I was just clearing up today and found this one. If it is not a trouble, could you please take it with you? But like I said, you can give it away if you prefer," she said handing over the jewellery that she had found earlier in the morning.

"I wouldn't and like I said, I would rather keep it as keepsake from you to remind me of you," Kavya said with a warm smile and pocketed the earrings in his suit jacket- the pair of earrings together after almost a year.

As she now looked at the manuscript, he had left behind, she could not bring herself to look into it. So, she left in the table and walked away lost in her thoughts.

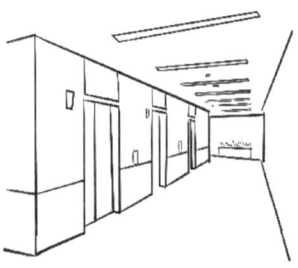

Chapter 22

Roman was entering the building carrying the parcel from the building lobby that had arrive for his wife. When he was walking towards the elevator, he bumped into Kavya. He was quite surprised at first to see Kavya there but soon enough he remembered the phone call from Kavya to Rajmati about delivering the book. *So, he did himself come to visit with the book,* Roman thought. Before they could greet each other, he noticed that the bizakani had dropped from Kavya's hand. Roman had remembered seeing photos of Rajmati with those earrings- almost all the photos of times he had missed in her life had her wearing those same pair of earrings, but he had never seen her wearing it once outside of those photos as long as they had been together. He might have seen her wearing it only once when he saw her at the dhungedhara but even then, he was more concerned toward the sadness in her eyes than what earring she was wearing. Now, seeing her earrings in his hand, made him wonder why *he* had her earrings with him.

164

"Kabiji, what a pleasant surprise to see you here," he greeted Kavya while his jaws tightened.

"It is a pleasure indeed. I just came to visit Rajmatiji and give her the book," Kavya replied unaware of the looming angst in Roman's voice.

"Oh, really, is it complete? I would love to read it too," Roman said as if he was not aware of the fact already.

"Please do and lend me your thoughts on it as she refuses to," Kavya's response making Roman's jealous heart settle a little. He was, however, still bothered to see her earrings in his hand. He thought it would be better to ask the owner of the earrings about it than the stranger in the lobby, so he replied, "Of course. OK. See you around," he said and moved towards the elevator.

When Roman opened the door, he saw the book lying on the coffee table and the name of book that held the name of his wife's name. His hands moved toward the book but retracted it upon hearing Rajmati's voice, "You are home early."

Rajmati smiled at him and took the box from his hand.

"Did you meet Kabiji, he just left?" she asked.

"Yeah, I met him and talked with him briefly," he said. Rajmati checked the label and placed the box in the floor while Roman went and sat in the couch.

"He also had your Bizakani," Roman said attempting a casual tone while trying to hide curiousness in his voice.

"Oh, yeah, I gave it to him as a thank you. I always wondered where I had lost the other pair of that earring but turns out he had it all along," she said laughing bringing her hand to the head. The gesture she usually did when she felt like what she did was stupid. Roman found that action rather cute. "Today when he brought it to return it, I decided to give him as a gift. I had parted my heart from it anyways so I thought he could just have it as a thank you." She then started moving upstairs towards their room while Roman followed her.

"But he is a man, what could he possibly do with those earrings? And didn't you like those earrings?" Roman inquired and for some reason her choice of word, 'parting away' with something she had worn for so long did not sit right with him. He wondered if there was any reason for her to let go of things. He then looked around and noticed there were variety of bags strewn across the floor, so he asked, "What are these bags for? Did you go to shopping or something?"

"No, these are all my things. I am giving some of it away-sort of like parting away with some of the stuff," she explained. Again, that word, *parting away. Why was she parting away with things? Is she not happy with current things?* he wondered and couldn't help but ask, "Why? Why are you parting away with your stuff?" His voice came out on a bit higher note than intended and noticing how taken aback she was by his inquiry, he lowered his tone, "I was just curious."

She then shrugged and said, "Just because. It was part of the past I did not want to do anything with. Some I don't use anymore and some don't fit me. I am just decluttering, Roman. Could you please help me bringing some of these downstairs." He nodded not really understanding or believing what she said. He did not know how to respond to it and only seemed more concerned by it.

Then they move back to the lounge area with both their hands full of bags and boxes. Once they put the bags down, he walked towards the coffee table and looking at the book in front of him, he asked, "Is this the book he wrote? He told me that you didn't want to read it."

"Oh yes, I was so excited when he first told me that he wanted to write something about me in his book. I mean, isn't it flattering? But now it is here I don't know if I want to read it."

"Why not? I mean it must be full of praises for you," Roman said.

She slowly nodded, "Yeah but not sure if I deserve it."

"Why would you say that?" Roman asked his previous concern now back at full swing and rising.

"I don't know," she shrugged.

"Raani, is everything really alright?" he asked, the question he asked her at least once in a day.

"Yes, everything is fine. Don't worry. I really need to rush to Tara's place before I go to work. Can we talk about this later?" she replied quickly. She had been avoiding talking about these things every time he had asked her if she was feeling ok and that only increased his concern over her.

"You can read the book, if you would like," she said before leaving out the door in rush. He couldn't even get a chance to ask why she had to rush to Tara's place.

He sat down and read the book but skipped directly to the title with her name on it. It was a ballad worth of 3 pages and probably the longest one in it. When reading that ballad, he felt upheaval of emotions. At one point he stood corrected about how he felt for her and what she was like while at the other end he felt like he was looking at his wife from a different perspective. He couldn't help but appreciate this stranger's words for his wife but not without a tinge of jealousy. The only thing he didn't like was the ending, so he put it in his mind to change it.

***

When she got back home, Roman was busy working on his laptop but his mind was still revolving around the words in the ballad about her. As much as he defined the beauty of hers, he also mentioned how luckless she was, how she got cheated out of her dreams. It troubled his mind and wondered if she was truly happy with him. Could this relationship be just a compromise for her? He was lost in thought so much that he did not realise that she was talking to him. He slightly raised his head from the laptop acknowledging her, "Sorry, I got caught up with the work. What were you saying?"

"I was just asking if you had seen the box that you had brought in earlier?" she asked. That question reminded him of the contents he had seen that package. She had been ordering several stuffs for the home and Roman had been helping with unpacking and storing them but unlike other times, this time the contents left him rather disturbed. It had several long ropes, some rat poisons— rest he could not process after seeing the first two. He had been distracted ever since, and all kinds of thoughts were shrouding his mind.

When he did not response, she asked again, "Did you open it?"

"Why? Should have I not open it?" he asked not looking up from laptop, while his mind still dwelling with possibilities about what would have happened if he had not opened it.

"It is fine if you have. It had the stuff I ordered for the bar. I mistakenly added home address instead of bar for that item and even forgot to take it with me earlier. I just wanted to check if you put it somewhere," she replied. For some reason, her explanation felt more unbelievable for his ears.

"Are you unhappy?" he blurted out.

"What? All I am looking for is that box," she replied with a look of shock colouring her face. She had been wanting to avoid him whenever he started asking such questions because it tended to change into a psychological session at times. A therapy session that she really didn't need but this time it felt different.

His anxiousness seemed to have taken over as he continued, "Life is beautiful, you should not give up on it. Talk to me if you feel something is not right. I will make sure to bring everything at your feet. Whatever you want but please-"

"Roman what's wrong?" she asked worried.

"Why don't you tell me what's wrong? I saw the contents of the box."

"What do you mean? It was just the box of ropes and some wall rings that I wanted to add to the bar for the aesthetic purposes. I noticed rat in the bookshop next door so I thought I would buy it for precaution. I have been ordering so many things for our house that this one also got here."

Her words suddenly brought clarity to his mind. She had shown him the new idea for the bar recently. Then he realised what he had just spoken so he said, "Sorry, I don't know what came on to me."

He then just moved towards their bedroom without any further word. Not wanting to take silence for an answer, she followed him, "Roman, what was that about?"

When he didn't say anything and just paced around the room pretending to look for something, it was now her time to ask him if everything was alright with him and she did, but he only nodded his head yes.

She then asked again, gently this time, "Is something bothering you?"

"No, it's nothing," he said now moving towards their bedroom window.

"It is not nothing Ro. Please talk to me. You have taken all my burden, share some of yours to me. Trust me with your demons. What are you so scared of? What got you so worried about the contents in that box?"

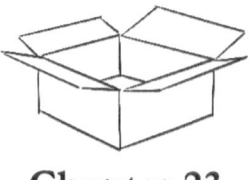

Chapter 23

"Why are you scared? What are you so scared of?" Rajmati asked Roman one more time. He stayed silent, looking outside of their bedroom window, staring at the night sky full of stars but no moon. At that very moment, it dawned to her what she had ordered, and what he had concluded it be for. *Why would he think that? Have I given him any reason to think that?* She thought. She walked towards him slowly and putting her left hand on his shoulder, she tugged him to look towards her. He stared down at her and at that very moment when their eyes met, she noticed how his beautiful amber eyes were glistening and how tortured they were.

Rajmati did not know how to talk to him about it. She had always thought that it must be his nature to worry but at times she wondered if there was some other reason. Rajmati had noticed number of times he would ask if she was fine or if she was ok even when she seemed to have not given any reason for him to worry about. It was endearing at times but confusing at other. Unable to withstand her swarming

171

emotions, the hurt she felt looking at his eyes tear up, she spoke again, making sure her own voice did not give up on her, "Hey, talk to me. I am not going to leave you. Me looking for solace is not to abandon you."

"I know. I know," he said removing her hand from his shoulders and holding them in his hands.

"Then, what is it? Talk to me. What's wrong?" she asked gently squeezing her palm onto his.

He raised his eyes slightly trying to look away from her so that he could say what he was going to say without looking at her, "I am scared that you would leave this world. I know you would not do such thing, but I cannot stop these thoughts from haunting me. I don't want to miss out on signs. Not again."

His words sucked the air out of her lungs. She had understood that he mistook the contents of box for something else, but it also left her wondering if she had ever given him any ideas to think that she would attempt anything as such. She stood by the window where wind blew past her curls while he moved towards the bed and sat on the edge of it with his both hands covering his face.

"Have you ever tried to—" she asked hesitantly not able to finish that sentence.

"No," he said shaking his head rather aggressively.

She walked towards the bed and sat beside him. One of them staring at wall and other at the floor. "You can talk to me, you know? About anything," she said turning her gaze from the forest green wall of their bedroom to him. He only nodded continuing his staring contest with the carpeted floor while she leaned her head onto his shoulder. Just when she thought it was only silence that he was going to exchange for her words, he spoke, "Do you remember Ratna? The friend you asked me about when we were sitting by the beach."

"Yeah, I do, you would usually play with him around the field when we were little," she said. She never got a chance to talk to him as much, but she had known about him. She used to see them both play around together at times but Roman never got a chance to introduce him to her.

"Yep, he is the one. We had been friends since we were in school. Whether it was bunking the class or running to Swayambhu early in the morning, we would do it together. He and I also had guitar lessons together, so we used to play our favourite songs and sing together. After leaving the tole, we lost contact and after social media came through, he reached out to me, and we started getting in touch all over again. I was glad that he reached out."

She did not know where this was going but for some reason, she was scared to know and her instincts were right because Roman's next words were, "I lost him to depression."

Chapter 24

Roman and Ratna were best friends. Roman did not like to make many friends so he would mostly hangout with Ratna at school and sometimes even after school. Rajmati was another person that another friend he had that he enjoyed spending time with.

From playing the songs in band together to doing pranks with their friends, Roman and Ratna were always together until one day when Roman had to leave Kathmandu. As Roman had to grew up in different cities at different times due to his father's occupation, he gradually learned to make more friends. He would always meet Ratna if he ever visited Kathmandu however such visits got lesser and lesser as time passed by and they eventually lost touch. Both had their own group of friends and circles they spend time with.

It was when Ratna sent a friend request to Roman one day, they started talking again and somehow their friendship carried on as if it continued right from where it was paused.

174

They caught up with one another via social media. Roman and his family soon moved back to Kathmandu permanently but Roman had to go to Sydney to complete his study. Roman tried to keep in touch with his friend but both of them got so busy with their lives that they hardly found a time to catch up. Soon from occasional "what's up" in the chat turned into "nice picture" in the comment to simple like or reaction in the post and eventually that also stopped because life happened.

Five years ago, Roman had returned from Sydney after completing his degree in real estate management. He might have gotten busy after going abroad but he had always remembered his friends so when he came back, he decided to catch up with everyone. Most of his school friends were in different parts of the world so he contacted them and planned a reunion. He looked for Rajmati as well, but he did not know what he would go and tell her, so he never approached her.

All of his friends had started working or were at the stage of finding new job or starting a business. Ratna was one of the hardest friends to get hold of among all his friends. At first, he thought that he must have been busy but when Ratna kept on dodging every plan he made with all their friends, he had had enough, so one day he decided to go to his house and meet him there.

"You are one busy person, Ratna. I tried to contact you so much since I arrived. You barely respond to my messages. All I get is, I'll try, seriously?"

"Sorry dude, I wanted to arrange time for us to meet but I am caught up with this new work I have started," he replied in sombre tone.

He was not expecting his friend to apologise or talk in a matter-of-fact way. He was used to doing banter with him like brothers do. He was expecting for him to say something like, *"Of course, I am busy. You should come and see me,"* and they both would laugh but there was no laughter- not even a sign of a smile. As so much time had passed, he assumed that's what adulthood does to a person and their friendship; there was no place for their usual banters. He thought no matter how old they became; they would always have their silly banters.

He then asked, "Ok, no need to be this serious but if you are really sorry, then we are going out to you must come to this new club that we are going. I don't know anything else."

"I don't know," his friend started.

"You need to relax my friend. You are working too much. I have come all the way here to invite you. You cannot decline my invite."

Ratna then finally agreed to join them, but he insisted that he would have to leave early.

As promised Ratna did join them at the club, surprising all the friends. It turned out that it was not only Roman he was avoiding. Ratna had not met any friends— even the friends who were all living in the same city. As all of them slowly started to get drunk, the "philosophical" drunken conversation also started to take place. Then it moved to politics a little and to their lives. Ratna kept on making jokes as he drank the night away and seemed to have let go his seriousness.

Then he suddenly turned toward Roman and said, "There is nothing here my friend. You should make something of yourself abroad. Don't listen to these morons."

"No, bud, there is so much potential. Market is new. You can do a lot. Don't listen to this depressed drunkard," the other friend said. The word *depressed* was thrown around as a joke a lot that night. Nobody thought much of it. They were all working adults- all of them were somewhat depressed one way or the other but none of them knew that one of their friends was suffering a severity of it.

After that night, the group of friends met several times for the time, but Ratna was mostly absent in these gatherings. Even on one of those gatherings where he did show up, he seemed to be mostly lost in thought and rarely said anything.

"Are you in love or something? Where are you lost?" Roman asked jokingly once. But instead of pushing him away and saying it was nothing like that, Ratna instead blurted out, "Life is getting tough, man."

"How so?" Roman asked.

"Work, life everything," Ratna shrugged.

"Do you need help with anything?" Roman asked genuinely.

"What do you think of yourself?" Ratna responded angrily, "Do you think your money can solve everything?"

"No, I didn't mean that. I just meant that I am there for you if you need anything," he tried to explain.

"Nah, none of you can do anything. You all are friends in name only."

"What is that supposed to mean? I have been trying to contact you ever since I came here but you prefer to hole up in your room. You don't even try, and I am the friend only for the sake of it?" Roman said his voice rising.

"I am not interested in any explanation. You all are blind-walking aimlessly in life trying to please your boss and running after the carrot like a donkey."

"What are you talking about?" Roman asked frustrated.

"Nothing," he said and walked away.

"Ratna, What the hell! Let's talk it out man."

"Leave me alone," Ratna shouted without looking back. Roman did not say anything and just walked away.

Roman did not think much of it because people would say such thing, *right?* People tend to say things they did not mean. *Maybe he was just frustrated at work. He will come around.*

Like Roman assumed Ratna did come around- not as quickly but he did. They did not address their earlier conversation and just carried on like nothing happened. One of their friends was getting married so they decided to prepare a surprise performance for their friend.

Roman was at home when Ratna visited him. He was there to practice their performance in which Roman was going to sing, and Ratna was playing guitar. They were rusty at beginning but slowly they got back to playing like they used to.

After rehearsal, Ratna took out something from his bag, then he handed it over to Roman. It was the first copy of "The Beatles" vinyl record that was imported to Nepal. It was one of the dearest things that Ratna held on to but now he was handing it over to Roman.

"Why are you giving me this?" Roman asked.

"You had always wanted it, I know. I can now part my way with it. As you will be leaving for Sydney again soon, I wanted to gift it to you," he said.

"Don't you need it?"

"How many times will I listen to it? I know you recently bought that vintage vinyl player so it would be perfect addition to your collection."

"So, you do follow my activity in the social media," he said.

"Isn't that why you post? To keep everyone updated on what is going on with your life ha-ha," he joked and both of them laughed. Roman thanked him for the gift and kept it aside.

After some time Ratna left, leaving behind his half-drunk cup of tea and untouched biscuit.

None of the friend group noticed it much but in retrospect, he would be lost somewhere in thought even when surrounded with friends. He would talk about money and materialism in a very random and weird way that they could not understand. It did not happen all at the same time either. One day he was happy talking with everyone, the next day he would disappear off the grid from everyone. None of the friend knew what was happening with him. He was the happiest of the group but suddenly he was not, and nobody thought most of it because everyone was in the new phase of adulting and struggling in their own way that watching out for a struggling friend fell on the blind spot.

It had been normal for him to be off the grid, so nobody thought much of it when he did not respond the last group call. Roman however had been rather worried about him though he would not admit that to his friend. Ratna had been rather reclusive and more serious than he used to be. So, he called him one night to ask him how he was doing. But he never picked up the call.

It was late summer night; the night air was chilly despite the heat of daytime. When he couldn't get hold him over the phone, he left him text message asking him if he wanted to catch up the next day but there was no response. Something did not feel right so he went to see him at his home.

When Roman reached Ratna's house, he saw that a huge crowd of people forming right outside and heard a sound of someone wailing and sirens blaring. Confused he looked around, trying to understand what was happening. Then, he saw his friend's mother, and also the source of the scream. He still could not comprehend what was happening. He looked for his friend's father and assumed if something had happened to him, then he looked for his friend to make sure how he was doing in this mess but not in any world, he had assumed that it would be his friend that he would see lying on the stretcher that was now being moved into the ambulance; lying motionless with no sign of life in his body. He saw the signs of his struggle and the cause of death— his neck lined with angry red marks left behind by the rope, the weapon he inflicted upon himself. He remembered every conversation with him that moment, all the signs he had missed out on, all the blind spots he moved past and all the hints he was giving, the silent whistle of help that he never heard. He wanted to scream, he wanted to bring him back, but he could not. He stood there wordless, voiceless. People pushed him away and he moved with the crowd, but he could not do anything voluntarily. He was too in shock to understand what had happened or to deal with the fact that the world he lived in does not have his friend— his best friend anymore. All the family members were crying at their loss while Ratna rested there amidst the noise unable to hear any of those screams, just like the rest of the world was when he was silently screaming. The aftermath of the world when it loses its gem— all the trauma passed along without any knowledge. Roman stood there for a long time unable to do anything. He could not cry, he could speak. He just stood there.

Ever since that day, he made a vow to never overlook such signs, not to ignore even the whisper of need.

"This seems to have made me over observant and overbearing at times without even realising," he said to Rajmati who had been sitting beside their bed listening to him, tears brimming in her eyes. He took a long breath and looked down at the floor.

She pulled him into a hug and said, "You can cry, you know. You had lost a friend. You are allowed to mourn him."

"Do I even deserve to do that?" he asked, his voice almost breaking.

"It was not your fault, Ro," she said looking at him, but he looked away. She then brought her both palms towards his

181

face and gently turning his head towards her, she said, "You can cry, you know. I will be right here to hold you. You did not cry then but you can today. You had lost your best friend. Please let it all out. Please don't punish yourself like this."

He was equal part surprised and equal part grateful to hear her say that. It was almost as if her words held the power of will, his tears made its way, and he sobbed like he had never before. He never cried even at the funeral. He had been in shock for so long, anxious, and worried for his loved ones for so long that he forgot to take care of himself. His cry was loud and full of hurt. She held onto him throughout his breakdown, stayed right by his side like she promised and cried with him— both of them now on the floor of their bedroom. As they found their breath after crying, they stayed on the floor in silence for a long time.

"Thank you," he said after a while, and he meant it.

"All of us cannot be saviour all the time even if we want to. It is a very heavy responsibility to impose on oneself," she said.

He nodded and after a moment he asked, "Can I ask you one thing, are you really happy in this relationship with me?" making her momentarily startled.

"Of course, I am Roman. You gave me a choice to leave you remember?" she reminded him, then she added, "You have become my safe haven, Roman, my home. I would not trade it for anything. Not even death, itself. You have become my everything."

"I will not let any harm come to you as long as I am here," he said holding her face softly between his palms.

182

"I know you would not. This marriage is not a ruse to save me from myself, was it? If so, let me tell you, you don't have to save me from me. If anything, you have to save yourself from me because I am here to stay," she said trying to lighten the mood.

"Promise?" he smiled.

"Promise," she added.

"I love you," he breathed. Those three words that he had already shown and said million times but for some reason, this time it sounded like a reverence.

"I love you too, so much," she expressed wholeheartedly as if it was the only thing she was meant to do.

Chapter 25

Colourful variety of flowers were blooming across the valley with the arrival of spring. With Fagu Purnima, just over, one could see the traces of the colour sprinkled across the street, result of colour thrown at each other during the celebration.

"Thank you for agreeing to meet me, Kabiji," Roman said sitting across the table opposite Kavya. He was curious about the ballad Kavya had written about Rajmati, so he had invited him at the restaurant near his workplace to talk further about it.

They were sitting in the outdoor setting of the restaurant overlooking the small garden where new buds of flower were slowly emerging. They were sitting in one of the antique chairs with a circular table between them. A big parasol was giving them shade from the sun. A chilly weather was getting slowly warmer with spring coming closer.

"Well, when a powerful man of the city invites you for a lunch, how can you possibly deny," Kavya responded with humour.

"You are the man of words. I would debate that you are the powerful one," Roman responded with a grin and proceeded to ask, "What would you prefer, coffee, tea?"

Kavya simply smiled and replied, "Tea, perhaps, perfect in this weather, what are you having?"

"Tea, it is," Roman made a polite hand gesture, and a young gentleman arrived in front of them to take their orders.

Once their orders were taken, server left leaving the two to carry on with their conversations.

"I read your book," Roman started.

"By that I believe, you only read the pages about your wife," Kavya said smirking.

"Well, none of the other titles were as enrapturing to be honest, what can I say?" Roman shrugged.

"I will not disagree. Do you have any comments or compliments regarding the ballad?" he asked curiously.

"Yes, for both," Roman said with serious tone, "I love your way with words Kabiji, I have always admired that. You might not believe me, but I have read your earlier works. The way you described my wife, it is beautiful, and I understand you would not hear that from any husband every now and then. I must also admit that I was envious of the choice of words you had used. I was angry, I confess. But may I ask why did you

185

present her to be luckless. Why would you make her ending so sad and unhappy?"

"Who says that was an ending? It was an ending to that ballad, yes but that is not her ending and when I saw her last time, she seemed happy and content, which is far from what that ballad says," Kavya responded calmly.

"I understand but why would you make it so sad," he asked, "was she sad?"

"Because people love tragedy perhaps. I don't know if she was truly sad. Her eyes rarely shone like they do now. I wrote what I saw in the past, the conversations I overheard between her and her friends, from people around the tole before and after she got married. So, I presumed it was not a happy situation but an arranged one. I assumed she was not happy at all after marrying you.

I cannot argue that it did not come from my own bitterness as well. Everyone wanted to have her and when you cannot have what you longed for, you give excuses for why you didn't want them just like that fox that claims the grapes must be bitter because he could not have it."

"Were you one of her suitors?" he asked.

"If you ask her, she will tell you, I never intended to marry her but that was a lie I told her. I had asked my father if I can marry her. He denied. I was not planning to ask her out, but she rejected me even before I tried so to keep my ego alive, I told her that I was in love with the idea of hers, which only now I believe it to be true— not at the time when I said it. I am man enough to accept that this ballad did have an essence of my own jealousy, but I was genuinely happy to see her recently at your penthouse, looking more beautiful than she ever was. I didn't even know that was possible. After returning home, I contemplated and realised that she looked content and for some reason I was content to see her that way. Thank you for bringing that happiness to her."

Roman did not know how to respond for a moment. Before he could say anything, their teas were brought to them along with some cake.

After taking a small sip from his cup of tea, Roman asked, "Did people really talk about her in such a way?"

"Art, poetry, fiction are the exaggeration of realities, we should not take it to our heart so literally. Yes, people talk about people who are better than them, prettier than them. They don't like to believe that people are blessed with everything. It shatters their mirror of illusion. They rather believe that pretty face does not equate better life, and they would rather feel pity for someone than feel happy for them," Kavya expressed. A moment later, he said, "The book has been approved for publication but if you prefer to have the ending changed, I can try."

Roman shook his head no and said, "People have tendency to ruin beautiful things. I would love to keep my life with my wife private. It can be the fiction you wrote about her so we can continue to live our life happily."

Kavya smiled at that and agreed with him taking another sip of his tea.

"So, she loved houses with *Sajhya:* huh?" Roman said changing the subject but still referring to the words in the ballad that suggested she wanted to have a home with Sajhya:, a traditional artistic window frame that used to be part of old architecture. It was thought to be a window from which lady would sit next to and comb their hair looking outside.

"I overheard her talking with her friends once. It makes sense, doesn't it? She loves using traditional motifs in her modern designs looking at how she designs places."

Roman simply nodded making a note in his mind that it did not matter if Kavya's muse didn't get everything she longed for because Rajmati will— she will get everything she ever wanted and more.

Chapter 26

Some truth frees us; some acceptances help forgive ourselves. Life is certainly a mix of all these little truths and acceptances. Once Rajmati was able to understand where Roman's anxiety was coming from, it helped her a lot to understand his concern. Suddenly, it was not suffocating, rather a chance to let him know that she was happy with him and how much she appreciated him.

She had been hyper-independent for so long that going to anyone asking for help was an exceedingly difficult task for her but with him it gradually became easy. Slowly with time, calling him and telling him about her day didn't feel cheesy, going to him about her problems didn't feel like being needy, being there for him and wanting to know more about him didn't feel like interrogating because eventually they realised that's what partnership was. Just like that they found each other all over again, filling the empty spaces in each part of their lives. She had promised to come and tell him whatever bothered her as long as he promised to do the same.

***

Bisket Jatra was recently over marking the start of a New Year and people were back to work and their mundane routine.

"Let's go on a weekend trip away from the city. What do you think?" Roman asked her, while they were sorting out their recent grocery purchases. Rajmati was putting away fruits and vegetables in the fridge while Roman was filling up the pantry. "Sounds good, is there anything in your mind?" she asked.

"How about our new house?" he said smiling at her.

Rajmati and Roman had purchased a modern two-storey house together on the outskirts of the city, elevated enough to offer a stunning view of the entire valley. It wasn't his or hers but a house to call their own. With both of their hard-earned savings invested in this property, they were determined to turn the house into a beautiful, cozy home. However, before moving in, some renovations were necessary. While there was not going to be any major changes to the exterior, they needed to ensure that the interior was liveable, and everything was secure and in order.

"We can go there, already? I thought we still have one more month to go before it is ready for us," she said looking surprised.

"There are few reparations that is still going on at the backyard and minor interior work is pending but it should not affect our stay," he said closing the upper cabinet.

"But shouldn't we go there only after we do ghar puja? It is an important ritual to do before we move into the house," she said.

"We are just visiting for couple of days, and we already did a small ritual when we purchased it remember so the main one, we will do it when we are officially moving in, how about that?" he reassured.

Closing the refrigerator door, she said, "That's great. I am excited to see how all the changes are looking."

"Yeah, I am excited for you to see the latest addition I made to the house," Roman said excitedly.

"What do you mean?" she asked surprised.

"Don't worry, it is not a big change. It is still the same house, just a tiny little addition. I hope you will love it."

"What change? What do you mean? Why didn't you tell me? I can't wait till then, please tell me now," Rajmati said, confusion and curiosity shrouding her mind.

"Sorry, Raani, it has to be a surprise," he said sneakily leaving Rajmati unsure of what he had done.

***

Their new house was about 1-hour drive from the valley. As they moved through the spiral, turns and curves of the hill, they finally reach the place. It had a beautiful entrance with exquisite front yard full of garden flowers blossoming and welcoming them. The pathway of the garden followed a beautiful two-storey brick house. Then her eyes landed on the uppermost floor of the house. It had an expansive terrace like balcony just as same as before but just cleaner and in better condition now and a little bit over to the side of the balcony, instead of a regular window, there was a 3 faced projecting window—intricately designed with traditional latticework.

Rajmati stumbled upon her words when her eyes fell on *Sajhya:*

When they were planning the renovation, adding such vintage bay window had been a passing thought in her mind but knowing Roman like the exterior of the house, she did not want to recommend any changes to it. She wanted to keep it the way he liked it despite knowing he would make that change if she ever so just mentioned it. She and Roman came up with different ideas for the interior of the house. "You are the expert, here," he would say and ticked off any thing she wanted to add.

Among all this redevelopment and working on their house project, he somehow managed to add something to the house that she had always wanted to have, without she ever needing to tell him. She was speechless.

What a thoughtful gift and a wonderful surprise.

"Oh my god. I can't believe it," she gasped, bringing both her hands to her face.

"So, do you like the surprise?" he whispered coming close to her.

"I love it," she said and turned around to hug him.

As they moved inside the house that opened to a spacious living area, chandelier in the ceiling and the curvy staircase connecting the upper floor, Rajmati was mesmerised. She was not able to visit as frequently as she wanted, to see how her vision was applied to the house because of a very demanding client she was working with, at that moment. She was nervous to see how it had turned out, but it seemed that Roman, despite his own busy schedule, made sure there was not a single compromise because the place was exactly how she envisioned it.

She sat by the small alcove of *sajhya:* and looked outside, from there she could see the garden of the house and the beautiful valley. Then she moved to the balcony, which was almost like a terrace overlooking the same view. There were a couple of outdoor chairs, a table, and a swinging chair at one corner.

She walked towards the railing of the balcony where Roman was standing. They both stood there watching the valley. Rajmati leaned her head on his shoulder, and he wrapped his arm around hers. A moment later he asked, "Do you like it here?"

"I love it. I am glad we bought this place," she replied.

He nodded in agreement, his arms now circling her waist.

After a moment, she said, "Thank you for adding sajhyaa. I love it."

He let go of her waist and turning her fully towards him now, he said, "Anything for my Raani."

"How could you possibly have known that? Did you talk to my friends?" she asked.

"I have my sources. I wanted to make this the home you always dreamt of living in."

"You are unbelievable," she exclaimed and hugged him.

He simply smiled, his eyes proud and full of love to be able to bring that to her.

"I have got something else as well," he said and went inside the room.

"What is it?" she asked from where she was standing.

"Just take a seat, I will be right back," he said and disappeared inside the house.

After a while he came back holding a throw blanket and two cups of tea. Putting the cups on the table, he handed her the blanket and moved inside again. This time when he came back, he was holding a guitar. He sat on a chair next to Rajmati who was now snuggled in a blanket with cup of tea on her hand. Rajmati looked at him with eyes full of love and warmth upon seeing the guitar in his hand. The instrument that he did not dare to touch for a very long time. She waited patiently as he tuned the strings. After some tuning and arranging, he started singing and strumming her favourite song in his melodious voice. She looked at him in awe and pure admiration. When he finished singing the song, her eyes teared up a little, cheeks turned red, and a beautiful smile graced her face. She then moved towards him and holding his face, she said, "Oh I love it. I love it so much. I love you so much."

"I love you more," he said seductively looking into her eyes and then looking away he teased, "But careful, now. You might have to listen to this every day."

"I am hoping to," she whispered moving closer towards him and kissed him on his lips. Slightly taken aback by gesture, he slowly deepened the kiss moving his hand around her waist while her hand moved over his hair.

The fresh wind was blowing around while the bright sun shone majestically in the sky. Two lovers were gleefully sitting by the Sajhya: soaking in the sun and enjoying the view. Few stolen glances, exchange of mischievous smile and one would know they were hopelessly in love with each other.

That day Roman said something that stayed with her for the rest of their lives, "They may not know your real story for they have only looked for the words they wanted to hear, answers they wanted to believe. But I will make sure that you are the happiest and luckiest of them all. I will give you tremendous amount of love so much so that it does not matter what the world thinks or believes. I will create a world to call our own and make you, its Queen."

THE END

About Author

Jenisha Manandhar was born and raised amidst the vibrant cultural tapestry of Kathmandu, Nepal, where she discovered her passion for storytelling at a young age. With an insatiable imagination and a deep appreciation for the power of words, she embarked on a journey to share her unique narratives with the world.

With her multicultural background and a keen eye for human emotions, she crafts narratives that resonate on a universal level. Currently residing in Sydney, Jenisha draws inspiration from the vibrant cityscape and diverse communities around her.

Books by Jenisha Manandhar

Lost Letters

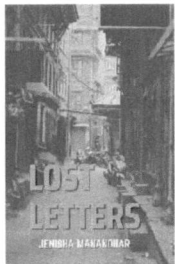

Moving Forward

Lumanti's Memory